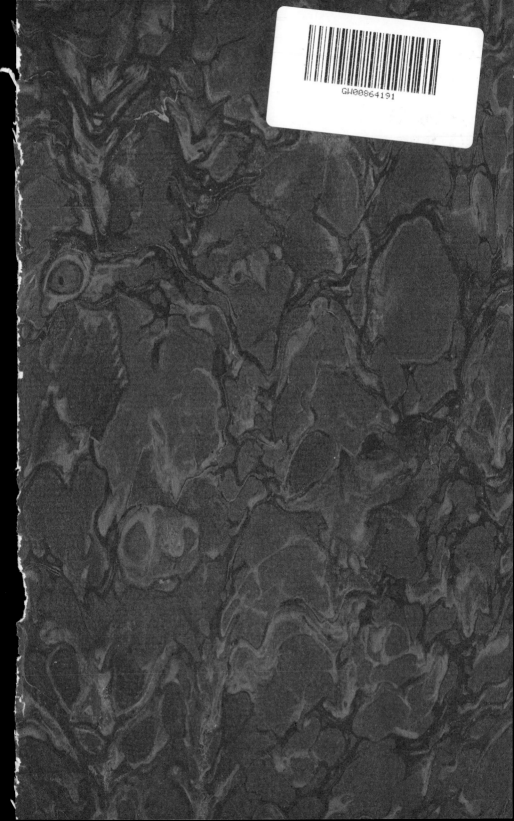

BOOK 1

TALES

OF THE TRULY GROTESQUE

THE STENCH OF SULPHUR SWAMP

BOOK 1
TALES
OF THE
TRULY GROTESQUE
THE STENCH OF SULPHUR SWAMP

annotated by
**Prof. Odysseus Malodorus,
B.S., M.S., Ph.D.**

illustrated by
Madame M

Published by Creepy Little Productions
Phoenix, Arizona

Library of Congress Control Number: 2005929175

ISBN 0-9704159-5-8

Printed in South Korea

First Edition
First Printing

Visit us on-line at:
www.trulygrotesque.com
www.creepylittlestories.com

TABLE OF CONTENTS

THE FISH STICK KING OF LOVE CANAL

Many moons ago, a fisherman slogged out along his trawler's frozen steel mast until he was leaning out over Love Canal. Icy daggers of rain bounced off his cracked yellow slicker and white-bearded face as he decided that, yes, it was finally time to end his life and jump into the eerily glowing, gray body of water.

This fisherman, who was known around the docks as Mr. Paul, was clearly unhappy. In fact, he was the single most unhappy fisherman on all seven of the high seas and all eleven of the lower canals. He had lost his first wife to a freak passenger seat airbag accident[1], and his second wife had fallen victim to a bad can of button mushrooms with botulism[2]. Not being one to dwell on his misfortunes, Mr. Paul took a third bride. This proved to be a fruitful union, and soon, Mr. Paul was the proud father of an apple-cheeked, dark-eyed, rotund baby girl.

Unfortunately for Mr. Paul, while his little girl was still a mere infant, she was kidnapped by a vicious gang of cotton-candy-hating, feral circus clowns[3]. After months of negotiations, Mr. Paul was unable to secure his daughter's release, and alas, soon thereafter, his lovely third wife abandoned him.

And if that wasn't bad enough, she abscond-

---

1. *You don't want to know the gory details, but let's just say Mr. Paul's first wife was not wearing her seatbelt or a crash helmet.*
2. *Hey, it happens. Not just to wives of Mr. Paul, but also to children who don't listen to their parents and eat without washing their hands first.*
3. *So, next time you see a clown wandering around your local mall, take my advice and head for the hills. Run! Fast! Hurry!*
4. *A fancy version of stealing that involves thievery, treachery, and a fishery.*

ed[4] with his secret fish stick recipe. This was a huge blow, because Mr. Paul had a horrible memory and only wrote the recipe down once, years earlier, on the back of a used facial tissue. And now, without his used tissue and/or his wife, Mr. Paul felt cursed, lost, and alone.

"Dagblammit![5]" Mr. Paul screamed to the heavens.

Of course, Mr. Paul could never forget how he'd coax all those little baby fishies into their small, rectangular homes, and then how he'd cheer for them as they grew into the perfect stick shape to fit side-by-side in those cardboard boxes found in the freezer sections of most supermarkets. But for the life of him, he could not remember the secret method he used to get all those salty-sweet, crunchy breadcrumbs to cling to the sides of the fishies. He had tried feeding breadcrumbs to his rectangular fishies, but that just left a crumby, sticky, fecal[6] residue

---

5. *Dagblammit is a nice way to say, Oh, Fudge To Yo' Mama!*
6. *Fecal is a nice way to say number two.*

on the bottom of his fish tanks and the shiny, naked fishies shivering in the cold water without their tasty, breadcrumb coats.

What was a poor fisherman to do? In this case, Mr. Paul reckoned that tossing himself into the deep blue sea was his best option. That then, is exactly why, at this very moment, Mr. Paul was throwing himself into the turbulent, icy, putrid waters of Love Canal.

Mr. Paul edged to the tip of the steel drag mast[7]. From where he stood, he could see nothing but gray water, gray clouds, gray rain. Yet, it's worth noting that life for Mr. Paul had not always been this gray. He used to be young and happy and filled with a certain *joi de vivre*[8]. At fish-fries all along Love Canal, he could regularly be found wearing lampshades on his head, juggling live floun-

---

7. *A trawler is not a sailing vessel, but it has large steel masts that drag otter boards and huge fishnets.*
8. *A French term that literally means joy of life, but really means being hap-hap-happy, which is a state of being that is foreign to most French speaking peoples!*

ders, and performing other wacky life-of-the-party[9] stunts.

Oh, what an appetite for life Mr. Paul once had! He thrilled at the stench of decaying, week-old catfish! He relished the deep, gurgling cry of two manatees cavorting at twelve fathoms! He loved the joy of slopping around barefoot in stinky fish heads, slimy fish guts, and bloodied salt water!

"Oo-la-la!" he'd exclaim as he munched on raw fish eyes, swirling them around in his mouth like sourballs. Soon he could take it no longer and he'd chomp-chomp-chomp on them until they burst onto his tongue with the salty-sweet flavor of squishy ocular[10] fluid. Of course, his greatest pleasure came from taking freshly chopped fish heads and putting them between two slices of soft Wonder

---

9. *It is commonly known that the single easiest way to become the life-of-the-party is to juggle live flounder and wear lampshades on your head, especially if you are a sailor.*
10. *Ocular means relating to the eye, and lest we forget, fish eyes are a surprisingly tasty delicacy in many nations.*

Bread, adding just a pinch of mayo, and... crunch-crunch! Yumm-o!

It was during this happy, but messy period of his life that Mr. P. felt compelled to come up with a new way to eat fish. And only a few weeks later, VOILA, he concocted the magnificent idea of stick-shaped fish. Yes, fish sticks were his brainchild. His! No one else's but his! His!! His!!!

Okay, yes, sure, Mr. P. was also the genius behind tartar sauce[11]. Yet, did he need credit for inventing the number one fish-related condiment? No! He was happy being known as the father of fish sticks and didn't care about the millions of dollars that were rightfully his from tartar sauce royalties[12]. He never really cared about money. He just wanted a wife or child to love, and maybe,

---

11. *Before Mr. Paul, no one had ever thought of scraping the tartar off their teeth and making a creamy sauce out of it.*
12. *These are the Mongol King and Queen of Tartar, who support their kingdom by making a few pennies every time you dip a piece of fried fish into a vat of tartar sauce.*

just maybe, to be loved as well.

But there was no love in his life, only loss. Mr. Paul had worked hard for many decades, and what did he have to show for it? Nothing. Nothing, except his creaky 47-foot trawler, which was constantly leaking and smelled of dead blowfish. Mr. Paul was a failure as a fisherman. The only thing he'd been able to catch all year was a cold. Mr. Paul was at the end of his 130-pound test, fluorocarbon, high-impact, monofilament[13] fishing line and ready to end it all by jumping into the cold, dark sea.

So, without further ado, he flung his body into the damp air... and waited for the brittle crack of his spine snapping as he hit the brutal, briny waves.

But there was no crack! No spinal snap! Only a soft whoosh as a huge gust of wind blew Mr. P. right back to where he had been standing just milliseconds earlier, on his

---

13. *Not to be confused with 129-pound monofilament, which is used only by amateur fishermen who don't know their ashtrays from their elbows...*

trawler's frozen steel mast.

Still depressed and now furious that he couldn't even succeed at killing himself, Mr. Paul shook his head and turned around. This time, with the wind at his back, he knew he would surely succeed.

Once again, Mr. Paul readied himself to jump. It was then, as he faced the other side of the canal for the first time all day, that Mr. Paul saw something strange...

A box. Bobbing on the water's surface. It was a shoe box, wrapped in a clear plastic bag. And there was a sound coming from the shoebox. A wailing. A crying. The box seemed to contain something which was alive.

What could it be? A new kind of wailing sea-shoe?

Mr. P. scurried down the mast and ran to the starboard side--or was it the port side? Mr. Paul was never very good at differentiating between the two sides of his boat. Either way, Mr. P. sprinted to the side closest to the floating box. He secured himself to the edge of the boat and reached out with the sharp tip of his fisherman's hook.

Now, fishermen's hooks are designed to impale fish, not gently scoop up boxes, so it was a tricky procedure. But even though he was not the world's greatest fisherman, he had not been out at sea for so many years without at least picking up some excellent hooking skills. Thus, with one graceful sweep of his arms, Mr. P. was able to hook the plastic handle of the bag holding the shoe box.

Ever so carefully, Mr. Paul eased the box closer and closer to his trawler. When it floated within arm's length, Mr. P. grabbed, the box, opened it and was finally able to see the contents.

It was a baby! A shivering pink infant

---

14. *The two sides of a boat are not called right or left, and if you call them that, the maritime police will arrest you and lock you up in a room with a dead octopus for eternity or even longer.*
15. *The main thing Mr. Paul knew about the sides of a boat is that one should never lean over either side and pee into the wind, because that's not very sanitary for you or the fishies.*

wrapped in a seaweedy-slick cloth. The winds of fate had rescued Mr. P. so that he might save this poor child. Maybe his life wasn't cursed after all.

Mr. Paul took the baby in his arms and hugged him. As he felt the baby's warm breath caress his cheek, he fantasized about raising the child as his own.

Yet, as Mr. Paul stared down at his precious cargo, he knew he couldn't keep the child. Surely, this baby's parents would be missing him something fierce. Keeping the infant would be a terribly selfish act. He had to track down the child's parents and give him back.

Mr. Paul motored straight back to the harbor. Once he docked his trawler and deboated[16], he searched everywhere for posted signs featuring pictures of the baby. He even went to the Love Canal Convenience Mart and looked on the back of all the milk cartons, but to no avail.

After several hours of futilely searching for the child's parents, Mr. Paul gave up and returned to his trawler with his newfound cargo. The child didn't seem to belong to anyone. He must be an orphan.

An orphan! Why hadn't he thought of that sooner?!! Mr. Paul picked up the sleeping babe and looked at him. Suddenly, the child spit out a trickle of seawater, laughed, and opened his sparkling sea-green eyes.

Mr. Paul was smitten. He completely forgot about losing his fish stick fortune. Suddenly, he had a new reason to live. He knew what he had to do...

Mr. Paul would raise this little boy as his own. He lifted the baby out of the shoebox and held him against his chest. Tiny droplets of baby vomit spurted out of the child's mouth and formed a foamy rivulet down Mr. P's cracked yellow slicker.

As he held the child, Mr. Paul felt a large lump

---

16. *This is like deplaning, derailing, or defacing, but from a boat and not from a plane, rail, or face.*
17. *The opposite of being plussed. People who are plussed are not affected by things and not good at math.*

in the baby's diapers. Ooh, the stench was worse than a ton of decaying chum and fish carcasses! For a tiny human being, this child had the potent digestive system of a large brontosaurus.

But Mr. Paul was nonplussed[17]. He brought the child and his shoebox down the stairs of the trawler and into the galley. Even if he only had been a father for a short time, Mr. Paul was still a master at diaper removal. As Mr. Paul slid the disposable diaper off the purpley-pink child, he noticed something. This baby didn't have male genitalia[18] like most boys.

In fact, this baby wasn't a boy at all. Mr. Paul had rescued a girl. A beautiful, little baby girl with five cute, little webbed fingers on each hand and five cute, little webbed toes on each foot.

Most people might have been disgusted or shocked by webbed feet and toes, but not Mr. Paul!

Mr. Paul was a fisherman. He had spent his life among web-footed creatures, and he admired their ability to move so effortlessly through the water. Mr. Paul firmly believed that, just because someone looked a little different or had a small peculiarity, such as webbed feet or hands, it was wrong to judge them. Mr. Paul knew that all human beings are grotesque in their own peculiar ways. Though many people might not have webbed feet, per se, most probably have some other abnormality, such as belly button lint balls or stinky, cheesy[19] armpits. As a result, people should not judge others; they should merely accept them for who they are and love them.

That is exactly what Mr. Paul did with the baby girl he'd fished from the ocean. He loved her as if she were[20] his

---

18. *Don't ask, you know.*
19. *Not phony or fake cheesy, but stringy mozzarella cheesy.*
20. *You would think this word should be was, but it is supposed to be were, because it is tense and rather subjunctive. If you don't believe me, ask your English teacher.*

own daughter.

One dilemma remained. What, oh what, would he call her? He knew this special child needed a special name.

Mr. Paul racked his brains, but still, he couldn't think of one decent name for his beautiful baby. As he stared at her cardboard shoe box, he noticed some words printed on the top: Joan & David.

He thought to himself, "Hmmm... David is a nice name. That's it! David!... Well, actually, David's not really a girl's name... Let's see... What about Joan? Hmmm... Yeah... Joan... Joan is a pretty name. I'll name her Joan!"

And that is how the green-eyed, web-toed, web-fingered baby in Mr. Paul's arms came to be known as Joan.

CHAPTER ONE
AN EXCELLENT, SUREFIRE, HUMUNGO PLAN

O nce Mr. Paul fished Joan out of the water, he carried her below deck and doted over her. Young Joan remained hidden in the belly of Mr. P.'s trawler for the next five years until it was finally time for her to attend kindergarten.

On that morning, Joan tied a pretty pink ribbon around each of her two pigtails. She put on her Mary Janes and a frilly pink dress that Mr. Paul had bought her. At 7:30 a.m., Mr. P. walked with her to the front of Love Canal Elementary School. As Mr. Paul watched her skip toward the front entrance, he felt certain she would enjoy getting an education and that her life was off to a fine start.

Yet, just as Joan waved good-bye to Mr. Paul, there was a collective GASP among the other schoolchildren.

Her hands. Her cute, little webbed hands. The other kids had noticed. They all stared. One even muttered, "Freak," under his breath.

Immediately, Joan shoved her hands under her armpits. With her arms crossed, she marched into the school building.

Six hours later, Mr. P. returned to retrieve his daughter. The moment Joan saw him, she jumped into his arms and wept deeply, her nose running and her tears rolling freely down his yellow slicker.

Between sobs, Joan exclaimed, "As God is my witness, I shall never set foot above deck again!"

And so, Joan dropped out of western civilization. In one fell swoop[21], she became the most shy and anti-social little girl in the world. She never returned to school, or for that matter, to any place above deck.

All day, every day, Joan remained below deck in her little book-lined nest. She threw out her pink dress and her Mary Janes, and from then on, wore only black boots, a black dress, a black elastic with black beads around each of her pigtails, and black cat-eye glasses with sparkling rhinestones embedded in the corners. Without these glasses, she could hardly see, but with them, she could read comfortably for hours and hours...

21. *Kind of like a big scoop of ice cream, but not a scoop, a swoop.*

Her daily routine never varied. From early morning to late at night, whenever she wasn't cleaning or cooking, she read books that Mr. P. either bought for her or checked out for her from the library. Joan turned herself into an autodidact[22] who was incredibly well-educated even though she had only attended one day of formal schooling. In addition, she rejected all forms of mass media, including radio, films, and even television!

As a result, by the time she turned thirteen, she was the only teenager in America who never used phrases such as, "Did you see that cool movie with like that cool actor, you know?," or "Slurpees give you brain freeze," or even "Hey, who took the freaking remote control?" In fact, her diction most resembled

---

22. *A self-taught person who never experiences the thrill of standing in line in the school cafeteria, only to have a fat, old lunch lady plop a spatula full of the mystery-meat-of-the-day onto her plate.*

a fifty-five-year-old Ph.D. in Nineteenth Century Russian Literature.

Joan relished her ritual of reading. She spent day after day tucked away in the back corner of the galley, her flashlight shining on one book[23] after another. Most young girls would have resented the fact that their room was right next to the fish storage area, but Joan was tolerant, kind-hearted, and most significantly, endowed with a weak sense of smell.

On the other hand, Joan had a very strong sense of touch. She loved the rough, cracked texture of old leather book covers. She relished running her fingers along the spines of all the books in her library, which she kept in perfect alphabetical order.

---

23. *In no particular order, her favorites were Gogol, Dostoyevsky, Malodorus, Nabokov (when he wasn't being naughty, i.e., Lolita), and Tolstoy.*

Many parents might have been disturbed by Joan's utter retreat from the world, but not Mr. Paul. He was grateful to have a healthy, happy child and respected her life choice to stay below deck.

Yet, Mr. Paul did have a feeling that after he was dead and gone, it was going to be very

hard for Joan to support herself if she never, ever came above deck. Of course, if he had not lost his fish stick empire, he might have been able to set up a trust fund for her, but alas, he was now completely broke.

The past thirteen years had been financially unsuccessful ones for Mr. Paul. He was so intent on being a good father, he had turned into an even more lackluster fisherman and was in deep debt[24].

Therefore, Mr. Paul obsessively attempted to devise a really good, surefire scheme; something even bigger than the invention of fish sticks and tartar sauce. A plan so excellent it would ensure that Joan would have her own little nest egg[25], allowing her to stay

---

24. *Similar to deep doo-doo, but not as squishy.*
25. *This might sound like a lovely breakfast entrée when scrambled, but it is really a large chunk of money that you should have in the bank for a rainy day.*

below deck for as long as she wanted or even longer. The problem was simply this – Mr. Paul couldn't think of anything ingeniously inventive or sure fire.

On the last day of autumn, when Mr. P. was at the end of his fishing line and had given up all hope, Joan tried to help out her dad. She went through her entire library, but could find nothing that seemed relevant. After hours of research, she finally stumbled across the May double issue of *Small Trawler Fisherman Monthly*. On page forty-two, Joan read a highly scientific article called, "Humungo in Hedsuk: How I Made a Mint Shrimping," written by the now-deceased, "Shrimpboat Bob" Orgovan. Excited, she called her father below deck.

Mr. Paul walked down the stairs and over to her. Joan waved the magazine in his face.

"Mr. Paul, please, you must read this article."

"Honey-bun, I'm busy obsessively attempting to devise a really good, surefire scheme. So please, just tell me what it says."

"The article states that there is a small town in Arkansas called Hedsuk, where there is a new strain of gargantuan, freshwater shrimp. These crustaceans[26], nicknamed 'Humungos,' were first sighted within the last year."

"Shmoopie-poo, c'mon now. Shrimp don't just appear out of thin air–"

"Affirmative. The genesis[27] of the Humungo can be traced to a certain Dr. Melvin Golem, who is founder and CEO of the world-famous Sulphur Swamp Language Laboratory of

---

26. *Shellfish which taste good in a crusty batter.*
27. *Genesis is a mid '70's art rock group and also the first and, some people claim, the best book of the Bible.*

Semiotics, Semantics, and Simians[28]. This scientist claims he bred them for a language experiment that failed, and so his son set them free in Sulphur Swamp."

"Hmmm. I do love shrimp cocktail... Hmmm-hmmm... If only we had a shrimp trawler."

"Ahem, sir, no disrespect intended, but sil vous plais[29], take a gander at this vessel upon which we stand—" Joan pointed at their trawler.

"Wait one cotton-picking minute! You're right! It's our lucky day! This boat could easily be used as a shrimp trawler, by golly! How big did you say those Humungos are?"

"The average Humungo weighs between

---

28. *Semiotics is the study of the idiotic uses of signs; semantics are wacky antics performed by Sam; and simians are apes that speak Latin.*
29. *Please in French. Also, sil vous plais has many more S's in it than necessary, but again, this is a function of it being French.*

five and ten pounds. Look, here's a photo-graph of Shrimpboat Bob holding an adult Hedsuk Humungo shrimp[30] that weighed over eight pounds."

She showed the photo to her dad. He took the picture, slipped on his glasses, and gasped! His eyes bulged, "Oh, my sweet Lord!"

Mr. Paul had found his excellent, sure-fire plan. Humungo shrimp farming was the answer to all his financial woes. He hugged Joan and screamed with delight.

Humungo in Hedsuk: How I Made a Mint in Shrimping!

---

30. *A shrimp implies smallness, and yet, this book claims there are Humungo shrimp, which would not be small, inherently by being Humungo. Trust me, dear reader, it will all make sense in the end.*

"My prayers have been answered! We're saved! Thank you, Suggie-Wuggie."

"My distinct pleasure." Joan beamed with pride.

Mr. P. paced around the galley, his once-blank mind now wild with thoughts. If Mr. P. knew anything, he knew that if he could raise crunchy batter covered Humungos, there was humungo money to be made. In only a few short years, Mr. Paul's Humungo batter-coated shrimp sticks would be sitting right next to his ex-wife's fish sticks in super-market freezer shelves across the country. Yes, he would be rich again, and little Joan would be set for life.

Mr. Paul heard the tempting siren song of crunchy Humungo sticks and knew they had to leave for Hedsuk at once.

Mr. Paul ran above deck, flicked on the

motorized anchor retrieval winching system, and revved up the engine. As the anchor came to rest on the deck, he turned the boat in the direction of Hedsuk[31].

As the trawler motored past the last familiar buoy in Love Canal and made its way on to the intracoastal waterway, Mr. Paul screamed, "Hedsuk, here we come!"

---

31. *Despite the common belief that Hedsuk is named after its foremost citizen, Buck Hedsuk, the truth is that this lovely town is really named after the habit of its villagers to suck the heads of crawfish in order to extract all the sweet skull juice.*

CHAPTER TWO

THE LAST OF THE REDNECKS

alfway around the world in the nation of Zimbabwe on the continent of Africa, sixteen year-old Emmett Golem was sick of traipsing through elephant grass and wanted to go home. Emmett did not like jungles. He was not African. In fact, he lived in Hedsuk, Arkansas, and was only in Africa because he was on safari with his father, a certain Dr. Melvin Golem. Yes, the same Dr. Melvin Golem[32] who had featured so promi-

---

32. *Duh! Of course this is the same guy. I mean, how many people do you know named Dr. Melvin Golem?*

nently in the Humungo shrimp article by "Shrimpboat Bob" Orgovan.

True, it was Emmett who had initially urged his father to take him to Africa, so they could capture the most intelligent of all primates[33]— the Redneck chimpanzee[34]. And yes, it was Emmett who yearned to bring back a Redneck to Hedsuk, train him in sign language, and show the world that even Rednecks could write great works of literature of a caliber equal to or maybe even a teensy-weensy bit better than Shakespeare.

Emmett could deny neither of these facts. But, still, his feet hurt from hiking all day long, he had lots of itchy insect bites, and he

---

33. *Yes, even more intelligent than Homo sapiens, which means wise man, but is really a misnomer, as demonstrated by the way Homo sapiens act these days.*
34. *Not to be confused with the human redneck, a different kind of primate, though with many similar attributes.*

was starving.

Emmett kicked at some elephant grass, "Dad, I'm tired. Can we go home now?"

"Not yet, Son. We're close. Real close. I can feel it."

"But Dad—"

"Emmett, my boy, have patience. All seventeen of the Rednecks left in the world live here in this trailer park/game reserve. Just keep keeping your eyes peeled."

"Yeah, but—"

"Look for an old pick-up truck on cinderblocks. That's a sure sign that you're close to one of their home-sites. And then, look carefully for a small primate with a glorious band of red hair around its neck."

"So, like why are they almost extinct?"

"Well, even though they are incredibly intelligent, this species is notoriously clumsy and afraid of heights. So, many Redneck chimps regularly fall out of tall trees and die. The other major cause of their shrinking numbers is the unanimous agreement among gourmets and gastronomists[35] that Redneck brain is by far the tastiest of all primate brains."

"Yuck!!!"

Of course, Emmett and his father had no intention of eating any Rednecks; they merely wanted to teach them how to speak in sign language and how to write like Shakespeare.

But even though he had the best of intentions, Emmett's feet were killing him and he couldn't take hiking around any longer. "Dad, we've been walking around in circles all day, and it's getting dark. We haven't heard even one Redneck yowl or screech. Can we turn

---

35. *People who dig food more than shopping or rock and roll.*

back now, please?"

"Alright... Fine..."

So, they turned around and marched back toward the small village at the edge of the jungle. As Emmett walked, his pale white skin glowed with perspiration. He was lean and muscular with sandy hair that hung in front of blue eyes, which he hid behind dark sunglasses. A nervous ball of energy, he had a habit of unconsciously tapping his feet and his hands. He was almost a foot taller than his father, though still just under six feet tall. Emmett had a bit of acne vulgaris[36] on his forehead, chronic gastritis[37], a nervous habit of flipping his long bangs out of his eyes, and a squeaky voice that cracked constantly.

---

36. *As opposed to acne politis, which is a much better-behaved form of acne.*
37. *A disease of the lower bowels in which a constant stream of fetid, noxious gas is emitted out the rectum.*

Because he was so self-conscious of his voice, Emmett preferred using Ameslan[38] (American Sign Language) to talking. He had learned Ameslan a few years earlier and had tried to teach it to the Humungo shrimp in the lab, but all his efforts had failed. However, whenever he got into fights with his father, he found Ameslan useful in that it allowed him to say nasty things behind his father's back and not get caught.

Emmett's father, Dr. Melvin Golem, was a short, hyperactive man with a bad comb-over, thick features, even thicker glasses, a khaki utility vest, khaki utility shorts, large hiking boots, and a bushy beard. Dr. Golem loved hiking and was disappointed that they had to

---

38. *Not to be confused with Ameslang, which is comprised of basic signs for swearing, like flicking one's teeth with one's thumb, and, of course, holding one's middle finger up in the air in order to imply nasty, naughty curses.*

turn back, but it was getting dark and he knew it was time to return to civilization.

"Well, we might've struck out today, but there's always tomorrow, right, kiddo?"

"Yeah, Dad. Sure."

Emmett also had a secret ulterior motive for wanting to take this trip. He and his father lived in the middle of nowhere, he had no brothers or sisters and no mother, and his father had forbidden him from going to school. So, now, Emmett's goal was to find a friend, preferably one who he could speak in sign language.

As he and his father marched back through the elephant grass, Emmett exclaimed, "Dad, when we get back to Hedsuk, do you think I can maybe go to school?"

Dr. Golem answered, "Look, kiddo. When you went to school, you had that horrible accident and you lost all memory of your first fourteen years, remember?"

"Yeah... I mean, no... I mean, if I have no memory of it, how could I remember?"

"That's not the point. The point is that in the two years that you've stayed home since then, have you had any horrible accidents?"

"No."

"See? I'm doing you a favor. Besides, how many kids get to live in their own state-of-the-art language lab and have fathers who are award-winning scientists?"

Melvin waited for a response. Emmett nervously tapped his thigh with his hand—and then responded in sign language.

His father glared at him. "No, speak to me with your tongue, not your hands!"

Emmett spurted out, "I don't know, dude... None?"

"Right-o! As any scientist worth his salt would then deduce, for a gifted kid like you, school is a total waste of time. In a classroom, you'd never get the superior education you're receiving being home-schooled."

"But I want to go. There are girls at—"

"Forget girls. They'll only bring you heartache and pain. And, anyway, schools are too dangerous these days. Why, I read that a lot of kids today bring metal detectors into school and hide them in their lockers next to their guns--"

"Dad. Listen to me! I—"

But before Emmett could finish his sentence, his father added, "Fine. Go to school. But don't come home to me, crying about how all the girls made fun of your voice and the rancid

---

39. *This was not a result of eating certain foodstuffs, such as baked beans or refried beans, but was a deadly symptom of chronic gastritis.*

emissions emanating from your buttocks.[39]"

"They won't make fun of me."

"Yes, they will. All children have the innate ability to intuitively figure out the exact things you are most sensitive about. Then, once they've found your Achilles heel[40], they'll prod and stab and puncture it until it's filled with puss and blood and you're rolling around the floor in horrible pain."

"That's gross, dude."

"I'm your dad, not your dude. And, of course, it's gross. We live in a horribly grotesque world."

"But-"

"No buts. Listen, son. It's just not worth it. When I was your age, I would've killed not to

---

40. *Your weakest spot, named after a Greek restaurateur, Achilles Lillios, who had a weakness for spinach pie and strained the back of his heel chasing after a run-away spinach pie in his restaurant.*

have to go to school. You're lucky. Trust me; you're better off being at home."

"Then, can I at least use the car to go out on weekends—"

"No! No, no, no! We have experiments to attend to, and I need your help in the lab."

"GOD!!! Whatever!" Emmett gave up.

Suddenly, a ferocious, screeching howl rang through the jungle. A Redneck howl. Instantly recognizing the sound, Emmett and his dad jumped up and down with glee. Then, they hightailed it out of the dense under-brush. They were getting close, but still, something felt wrong. The howl wasn't com-ing from the jungle; it was coming from the tiny village at the jungle's edge. How could that be? There was nothing in that little town but a few huts and a small eatery called the Laughing Monkey.

The only reasonable explanation Emmett could come up with was, well, that maybe the Redneck had gone into town to eat dinner at the Laughing Monkey...

CHAPTER THREE
THE MOST TRULY GROTESQUE RESTAURANT EVER

The truth was the Redneck had not gone into town to eat dinner at the Laughing Monkey; instead, he had been drugged and dragged into town to be eaten as dinner at the Laughing Monkey. And now he was tied to a silver serving cart in the kitchen, howling hysterically and making deep, guttural monkey noises as he was about to be served up as din-din!

Realizing the Redneck's yowls were screams for help, Emmett and his father ran as fast as they could toward the restaurant.

As they did, they prayed they would get there before only 16 Rednecks were left in the world.

You see, at that very moment, Lazlo Bleak, the world's greatest pencil-neck geek, flea circus ringmaster, and side-show impresario, was inside the Laughing Monkey, standing next to a large, round table with a small circular hole in its center. Four strange-looking individuals sat around the table; Lazlo towered above them, holding a long, flat, sharp steel blade that he had just pulled out of his thigh-holster. As they waited for dinner to be served, Lazlo sliced the air, practicing the move he would use to slash open the skull and expose the slick, juicy brains of the tasty young Redneck.

Since he was a geek, Lazlo loved eating live animals, especially chickens and Redneck

chimps. Lazlo had flown all the way from his home in French Lick, Indiana, to Zimbabwe to feast on live Redneck, and he was so excited that he was already salivating. As Lazlo swished his blade through the air, light shined off his huge, glorious, pomade-covered black pompadour. Remarkably tall, with thick thighs, a massive barrel chest, broad shoulders, and long, thin fingers, Lazlo cut a striking figure. More remarkable still, Lazlo never sweated, even though it was very hot and he was dressed all in black—black leather boots, black trousers, a black T-shirt, a long black jacket, and black leather gloves[41].

Lazlo also had a speech defect. This is not to equate speech defects with malignant personalities. In fact, many of the most heroic and benign[42] figures throughout history have had speech inconsistencies[43]. Simply put, Lazlo happened to slur some of his consonants, to stretch out words that didn't need to be stretched, and to spit a lot when he spoke.

As if spitting on people as he made them wait for him to finish a sentence wasn't bad enough, Lazlo also took great pleasure in raining on people's parades. In fact, there are several documented cases of Lazlo renting a

---

41. Lazlo was a PIB—which means a person in black. This type of primate is common in Manhattan or LA, but it rarely seen in the 110 degree heat of Africa.
42. The G is silent, in a good way. Think B-7, B-8, and then B-9.
43. King Arthur had a problem with his R's and called himself, Awthuw, etc.

crop duster, flying over a small town parade, seeding the clouds with rain pellets–setting off a huge rainstorm—and then laughing wickedly as he flew away.

The four people (if you can call them that) gathered together at the restaurant with Lazlo that day were his most trusted side-show curiosities[44] and cronies[45]. Though each was truly grotesque, Lazlo secretly dreamed of adding another attraction to his posse of human oddballs. A female freak, to be exact. Someone younger and prettier, yet still monstrous in her own special way. Then, and only then, would Lazlo finally have a complete set of side-show freaks and be completely content.

---

44. In addition to being his most trusted colleagues, they were also his only side-show curiosities.
45. You can tell if someone is good or bad by the name of the group of people who follow them. If they are good, they are followed by a team, like Team Molodorus, LLC, but if they are bad, they are followed by cronies, cohorts, gangs, accomplices, or denizens.

The person seated to Lazlo's immediate right was Queen Fleopatra, a raven-haired Egyptian beauty who could speak the language of fleas and command them to form any shape she desired. At all times, Fleo (as she is known to her enemies, being as she has no friends) wore a huge army of swarming fleas around her head, like a sort of turban. When Fleo was a child, her family was so poor that all her parents could afford to give her for her seventh birthday was a pair of fleas. The rest, as they say, is history.

Bouncing next to Fleo was a real troublemaker. Known by the name of Bobo

Biscuit, the Bouncing Boy of Borneo, this dark-hearted young fellow epitomized the word "round." He had a round, bald head; round, large, dark eyes; and a round, protruding tummy. Bobo's father was a snake charmer/yogi[46], which is where he got his flexibility, but it was from his maternal side that he got his unique bone structure. Bobo's mother hailed from a part of Borneo that is filled with rubber plants, and that is all she ate her whole life. Hence, unlike some contortionists who are double-jointed, Bobo was triple-jointed. In fact, his muscles and bones were all completely rubberized, so instead of just being incredibly flexible, he was also quite bouncible.

In the seat next to Bobo was a fierce-looking

---

46. *If you ever bump into Bobo's father, don't ever mention Bobo to him, or he just might sic his snake on you. I know; I have the fang scars to prove it.*

individual holding a bullwhip. At first glance, most people would assume that this freak in a one-piece, red leather outfit with metal studs was the side-show strongman. But this was no strongman--it was none other than Marooshka Ooofka, a Ukranian-born bearded lady/strongwoman. Hailing from a family of nuclear scientists and Olympic weightlifters, Marooshka had been a radiant, if rather beefy and hairy, child. And she had grown into a rather glowing, totally buffed, amazingly furry she-male. Now, most women prefer to wax or shave or zap their body hair; not Marooshka. Weighing in at over 200 pound of pure, rippling muscle, she dared anyone to so much as suggest she try electrolysis[47].

To her credit, Marooshka did not live in hirsute[48] shame. In fact, she loved her beard

---

47. *A process that removes hair and, in some cases, severe depression.*

and braided it, just like she braided the hair grow- ing out of her armpits. Not that it did anything to improve her personality. Foul-tempered and sadistic by nature, Marooshka thoroughly enjoyed admin- istering pain, especially cracking her whip against the bottoms of young boys and girls[49].

The fourth of Lazlo's grotesque comrades- in-harm was a dark-skinned, suave-looking, short man named Don Juan Frijoles. Don

---

48. *Yep, you guessed it. To be covered in her suit of hair.*
49. *If you ever meet her, I sincerely hope you do not stare at her facial hair and make a joke about her resemblance to Abe Lincoln, because if you do, you will surely face the wrath of her whip and receive a severe lashing.*

Juan claimed to be the direct descendant of Quetzelcoatl, the Aztec, feathered serpent of Mexico, but really, he was from Queens, New York, and just happened to have been born with a tail and feathers on his back and arms. Don Juan thought of himself as the world's greatest lover, but, in fact, The Don[50] had never been able to maintain a successful long-term, or even short-term, relationship.

This then was the nefarious coterie[51] of freaks seated around the circular table at the infamous Laughing Monkey Restaurant. This eatery was tiny and out of the way for a good reason. It only served rare, illegal dishes made out of endangered animals, such as Snow Leopard Scampi[52], Siberian Tiger ala Mode[53], and most significantly, the chef's special, the

---

50. *He likes to refer to himself in the third person as The Don. He thinks this makes him sound more formidable.*
51. *A nefarious coterie is like saying an evil gang, but with bigger words.*

dreaded live Redneck chimpanzee brain dinner, which is eaten with chilled soupspoons.

The head chef of the Laughing Monkey, a tiny albino man in a white apron and a big, white, puffy chef's hat, appeared from out of the kitchen, pushing a large silver cart toward the unsavory, salivating group at the round table. On the cart was the baby Redneck, tied down and howling in fear. The Redneck's yowl was so ferocious that it pierced the jungle air and could be heard by Emmett and Dr. Golem who were still running towards the restaurant.

Clenching the chilled soupspoons in their clammy fists and banging them on the table,

---

52. *Scampi is a nice way to say you are going to have really bad garlic burps for a few days.*
53. *Most people think a'la mode means with ice cream on top, and there are times when this may be true, but Tiger A'la Mode is always prepared with pepperoni chip sorbet, and it is quite yummy.*

the four freaks chanted in unison, "Redneck, Redneck, Redneck![54]"

Lazlo raised his knife high in the air and smiled at the bound Redneck. Just as his hand tightened around the handle to make the first cut[55] in the skull of the poor, little chimp, Emmett burst through the restaurant's swinging doors.

Immediately sizing up the situation, Emmett yelled, "Dad, grab the chef! I'll get the Redneck!"

Emmett and his dad leaped into action. Dr. Golem knocked over the little chef and snatched the cart, while Emmett untied the crying baby chimp and scooped him up in his arms.

Lazlo Bleak jumped out of his seat. He growled and stabbed at Emmett who stepped

54. *Among the rude and ill-mannered, this is a sure sign that one is hungry.*
55. *The first cut is also always the deepest.*

back away from him. The other freaks started to stand up, but before they could, Lazlo snarled and flicked his blade, signaling them to stay seated. Then, Lazlo smiled, stepped softly toward Emmett, and in the sweetest voice he could muster, he asked, "Dear boy, I'ddd invite you to joinnn usss, but I fearrr there's nottt enough sweetmeattt. So now, if you'd be so kinddd as to returnnn our dinner to usss!"

Terrified, Emmett stammered, "Uhh, ah, umm—"

Dr. Golem stepped forward and spoke for his son, "We're here to liberate this endangered species in the name of the Sulphur Swamp Language Laboratory of Semiotics, Semantics, and Simians." As he spoke, Dr. Golem reached for something in his pants.

Don Juan's tail flicked toward Melvin Golem. Fleo's swarm of fleas made an eerie, high-pitched buzz, shattering her empty water glass. Bobo bounced in his seat. Marooshka hissed. Emmett looked at them all and let out a yelp.

Dr. Golem froze. Then, slowly, ever so slowly, he pulled his wallet out of his khaki utility shorts, opened it, and drew out a large wad of greenbacks. Cold, hard cash. Lots of it. Suddenly, the dark, dangerous eyes of Lazlo seemed to soften.

Dr. Golem spoke in a frantic tone, "Please. I'll pay any amount. Just let us have the chimp!"

Lazlo returned his knife to its sheath. "Well, let'sss justtt see how much you are prepareddd to offer?"

Lazlo grabbed all the bills out of Dr. Golem's fingers, and counted the money. Then, he yanked the scientist's wallet out of his stubby fingers. Lazlo pulled out Dr. Golem's traveler's checks, credit cards, phone cards, family photos, and a piece of paper with a fortune on it from an old fortune cookie. Once Lazlo had every last thing of value, he handed the empty leather wallet back to Dr. Golem.

Dr. Golem thrust the wallet back into his pants and said, "Okay, fine. Keep it all. As long as we get the chimp."

Lazlo parted his lips, "Fine... Now, get out of my sssight. I'ddd like a little peace and quiet while I eattt my dinnerrr."

Dr. Golem nodded at Emmett, and they turned to get out of there as quickly as possible. The baby chimp and Emmett held each other tightly as they moved away from this strange man and his four dastardly accomplices.

Phewww! Just as Emmett wiped his brow with relief, Lazlo signaled to Fleo. She gave a command in ancient Egyptian, "Ooshkanazi, dallywoop!"

Suddenly, shwooomp! A swarm of fleas flew across the room and circled Emmett's head. Scared and temporarily blinded, Emmett and the baby chimp let go of each other. At that instant, Don Juan Frijoles' scaly tail struck out and swept Emmett's legs out from underneath him.

Emmett fell hard, hitting his head on the wooden floor. A bunch of rusty nails stuck up from the floorboards, but even though his forehead smashed directly into the pointed, rusty ends of the nails, they did not puncture the skin and there was no blood. In fact, it seemed as though his head flattened the nails against the floorboards.

As Emmett rubbed his head and wailed in pain, Bobo bounced up and grabbed the chimp who was now hanging from a light fixture.

"Stop! Freeze! Dr. Golem yelled, as he pulled a little can of mace out of his utility vest and pointed it at them. "Now, hand me back the chimp."

Just then, Marooshka flicked her bullwhip, knocking the mace out of his hand and sending the small man onto the ground. Dr. Golem sat there stunned, holding his wounded hand.

As Lazlo reached down with his long fingers to retrieve the baby chimp, Emmett let out a powerful wail, "Noooooooooo-ooooooooooooooo!" It was an unearthly sound, not altogether human. Like the rumble of an earthquake, it was a deeply resonating, high-frequency shriek that jarred the floors and rattled the windows.

As soon as he heard his son's wailing, Dr. Golem instinctively reached into his utility vest for his ultra-sonic earplugs, and he placed them in his ears[56]. This saved Dr. G. from the intense pain and severe hearing damage that the others were now experiencing.

In fact, even though Lazlo and his gang tried to cover their ears with their hands, they couldn't stop the pain or stem the flow of blood spurting out of their ear canals.

Emmett rose to his feet and continued to shriek fiercely, sending Lazlo and his cronies to their knees in eardrum-piercing, head-splitting pain.

"Noooooooooooooooooooooooooooo!" Emmett kept wailing as he helped his father to his feet with one hand while grabbing the baby chimp with the other. Then, holding the Redneck securely in his arms, Emmett and his dad stepped out of that horrible restaurant

---

56. *Having conducted so many lab experiments with sound, Dr. G. always carried a pair with him at all times...*

and out into the night air.

Too incapacitated with pain to follow them, Lazlo and his cronies lay on the restaurant floor moaning, groaning, and rolling around. It took a good ten minutes for the freakish thugs to finally collect themselves. By then, Dr. Golem, Emmett, and the baby Redneck were long gone.

Lazlo was furious. He had a killer headache. Blood had spilled on his nice, new black outfit. And he was starving. Never before had anybody crossed Lazlo Bleak and survived. Lazlo raised his gloved fist in the air, waved it around in small circles, and vowed, "Nobody interruptsss my dinner and getsss away with ittt! Thattt boy and hisss father will pay! Markkk my wordsss, they will payyy!"

CHAPTER FOUR

GOING ABOVE DECK, FINALLY

After weeks of sailing down the Eastern seaboard, Mr. Paul grew deeply concerned. Would there by any Humungos left by the time they finally got to Sulphur Swamp? What if Sulphur Swamp was all shrimped out? What would they do then?

Mr. Paul decided it was time to go below deck and discuss these pressing issues with the brains of the family--Joan. She would know what to do. She was educated. Okay, yes, self-educated, but still, a great deal more book-smart than this crusty old fisherman.

When Mr. P. reached the bottom landing, he gazed in wonder at his trusty young ward, sitting in her corner, curled around a book and a bag of carrot sticks[57]. He admired the intelligent and articulate young woman she had become, even if she appeared a bit pale and sickly from a lack of sunlight. When he really thought about it, he realized that the 13 years he'd spent raising and loving Joan had been the happiest of his mostly miserable life.

Silhouetted in the glow of her flashlight, Joan appeared small for a thirteen-year old. Wiry and fragile, she had skinny arms and legs that looked like pretzel sticks, big green eyes, and two black pigtails. As she read Dostoyevsky's *Crime and Punishment*, her face was fixed in a serious demeanor[58].

---

57. *After reading George Bernard Shaw, Joan became a vegetarian.*

Though she was not an unhappy child, she rarely flashed her big white, toothy smile or wasted time on frivolous joy and recreation[59]. When not cooking or cleaning, she donned her thick, black, cat-eye glasses and read books.

Joan sensed Mr. Paul wanted to chat with her, so she placed her bookmark on the open page and eased the novel onto her lap. She looked up at her father and smiled beatifically[60].

Mr. Paul smiled back and said, "Hey, veggie-wedgie[61], you ready for a great adventure?"

Joan cleared her throat and said, "Yes, sir."

"Well, eh, since you are first mate on this here trawler, I was wondering if you had any thoughts about the course I have set?"

---

58. *Da more you disturbed her while she read, da meaner she got.*
59. *Silly little things like frivols 'n bits.*
60. *This means peacefully and blissfully.*
61. *A term of endearment, which, literally translated, means my little asparagus.*

"Actually, Mr. Paul, no offense intended, but I do. Sil vous plais, hear me out... Have you, well, carefully thought through this trip to Hedsuk?"

"Of course, Sugar-Wooger."

"Because, unless all the maps I have perused over the past few weeks are inaccurate, the state of Arkansas is landlocked. And thus, hence, ergo, and therefore, it is physically impossible for us to get there on our trawler—which is, after all, a water-bound vessel."

"Oh, I never thought about that... Hmmm..." Mr. Paul decided that this was probably not the best time to bring up the issue of whether Sulphur Swamp was fished out or not. "Well, we'll find a way to get there, Itty-Bit, and you never know; things change. Maybe there will be a flood or something. Don't worry your pretty little head about it,

Boopie-doo."

He gave her a playful little punch to the shoulder and went back above deck. Joan wished she could help and racked her brain[62] trying to come up with a solution, but nothing came immediately to mind. Finally, Joan reckoned she'd figure something out before they got there. Then, she turned her attention back to Dostoyevsky.

After 40 days and 40 nights at sea, Mr. Paul docked the trawler in Hackberry on the Louisiana coast. This was as close as they would be able to get to Hedsuk by boat. Four hundred miles of land stood between them and Sulphur Swamp. There were no reports of floods on the horizon, and neither one of them had a driver's license, so they couldn't rent a

---

62. *It sounds like this means to take your brain out and put it on a rack, but, in fact, it merely means to think really hard.*

car. All they could do was wait for a miracle....

And wait...

And wait...

And so they did. For six whole days they waited. The whole time, neither Joan nor her father could come up with a good idea of how they were supposed to journey the last four hundred miles. Until, on the morning of the seventh day, Mr. Paul jumped out of the boat and onto the dock. He finally had a good idea.

"Land-boat! I'll make me a dagblam whale of a land-boat!" He grabbed some old car tires sitting on the dock, fastened them to the bottom of the boat, and tried turning the ship's wheel as if it were a steering wheel. Alas, the tires didn't turn. Mr. Paul threw himself belly-down on the deck of the ship, and wailed, "Woe is me. Me is woe!"

Mr. P. was plumb out of good ideas. He and

Joan would be stuck in Hackberry for what looked like forever, or at least a long, long time. In utter frustration, Mr. Paul wept a river of tears and banged on the trawler's deck.

The banging on the deck was so loud it interrupted Joan's reading. She looked up at the ceiling, shook her head, and sighed. Sure, Joan might have been anti-social and maybe even a bit socially retarded[63], but she was not one to give up easily in the face of adversity. Especially if her efforts could aid the kind soul sprawled in agony on the trawler's deck. Mr. Paul had cared for her all of her life; it was time for her to give a little back[64].

---

63. *This does not mean that if she were to take a bus to school, it would be the short bus; this means her social skills were less developed than that of your average 13 year old, which she clearly wasn't.*
64. *Growing up is mainly about realizing that you are not the center of the world. Yes, you are not the center of the world. Sorry, but it's true. Get over it and grow up!*

Yes, Joan was stuck below deck on the horns of a great dilemma. She had absolutely no desire to go above deck, but her father was on the verge of a nervous breakdown and needed help. Furthermore, she had done much research, but still, she had no idea how they were supposed to travel overland for the last 400 miles of their journey. And if that wasn't bad enough, she had run out of fresh food in the galley and new books in the library. Usually, her father took care of these essential necessities of life, but lately, he had become so obsessed with Humungos that he had ignored everything else.

Joan was torn. And she was deeply, deeply irked. The kind of irk that went way beyond her average, everyday state of irk. In fact, she was so extremely irked that, despite having vowed never to leave her cozy sanctuary below deck, she was suddenly preoccupied with strange fantasies about going above deck.

She tried to rid herself of such tomfoolery[65], but couldn't. In the same way her father suddenly become fixated with Humungo shrimp, she was now consumed with thoughts of going above deck to help him. Though she tried to repress these thoughts, she could not focus on anything else. She was obsessed with the idea of journeying above deck.

The whole concept of going above deck was outlandish[66], crazy, totally insane. She knew all the way down to the core of her being that she'd find only pain and hardship above deck. Above deck, people regularly suffered heart-

---

65. Another word for nonsense, derived from the now-deceased Irishman known as Tom O'Fooleri, who loved to suck his thumb and stick it into electrical sockets.
66. Really far out, man.

break, humiliation, death, and worse. She needed to stay put–right where she was, in the comfort and safety of her dark, cushioned sanctuary below deck.

Still, the gnawing[67] desire haunted her. A voice whispered in her head, "Go above deck, Joan. Help your poor old dad. Soak in the sun. Get some fresh food. Maybe even a few new paperbacks."

But she knew she shouldn't. She couldn't. It was sheer madness. Joan hadn't gone above deck in a good eight years. Why start now?

Yet, she had to consider the possibility. Things were different now. They were no longer in Love Canal. Her father was losing his mind, rolling around on the trawler's deck, muttering, "A whale of a land-boat!

---

67. *The initial G is silent, and doesn't that just gnaw at you?*

LAND-BOAT! LAND-BOAT!"

This was a state of emergency. She had to take charge. She had to go above deck. At least, that's what her mature, rational self said. But, her brain was saying something altogether different—imploring her to ignore this strange new desire and not to leave her refuge. She could almost hear her brain's voice plead, "Joan, Joan. What has gotten into you? Don't listen to that other voice. Don't go! There is nothing out there but mean, horrible people who will cause you pain and sorrow. Don't do it!"

What was she to do? She was in a bind. A real fix. Something or someone had to give, or she and Mr. P would surely starve—or go mad—or both.

Joan had to make a decision. A big decision. Maybe the biggest of her life. Definitely

the biggest since she'd decided to go below
deck eight years earlier.

Joan did not take decision-making lightly.
Oh, contraire! She pondered and postulated.
She considered and reconsidered all aspects
of her dilemma. After mulling and swishing it
all over in her mind, an answer finally for-
mulated and grew increasingly clear in her
head. Hard as she tried to deny and suppress
it, it would not disappear. It was the right
thing to do. Her only real choice...

Joan had to go above deck.

Yes, it was time. Mr. Paul had sacrificed
everything for her for 13 years; now she had
to do something for him. It was the mature,
responsible, and correct thing to do.

She would do it. She would go above deck.

She reassured herself that it would be for
only an incredibly short period of time. She

would go above deck for a few minutes, just long enough to help Mr. P. pull himself together and to grab a few books[68] and a little food. Then she would return immediately to her cozy home below deck. Surely, she'd be able to run out and do what she had to do and get back before anybody even noticed. And if they did, she had a good excuse: She and her father were on vacation. The regular rules of daily life don't apply on vacation[69].

Joan poked her head out from below deck. She squinted from the harsh sunlight scalding her eyes. She looked over at Mr. Paul. He was so busy muttering "LAND-BOAT, LAND-BOAT," and smashing his fists and feet into the wooden deck that he didn't even notice her.

---

68. *Most likely books by Prof. Odysseus Malodorus.*
69. *In Miss Manner's Guide to Etiquette, it clearly states that the regular rules don't apply to one on vacation. However, the moment vacation is over, they apply once again.*

Joan lifted her right foot off the top step and she tentatively inched her boot toward the deck.

Then, she quickly pulled it back. She couldn't do it.

NO! She had to do this.

Joan gathered all her courage and exhaled loudly. She lifted her right foot up again and thrust it forward. It swept through the air and touched down on one of the deck's wooden planks. As it landed on the surface of the deck, it didn't explode. Phew! What a relief!

She could do this. She took another step. Then another.

Now fully and completely above deck, she glanced over at her father for his reaction, but he was still so busy with his temper-tantrum that he didn't even see her, even though she was standing just inches away from him.

Finally, Joan grew reckless and muttered, "Um, eh, Mr. Paul—I mean, Pops—may I have permission to venture forth into the great unknown of Hackberry proper to scavenge for literary material and fresh comestibles[70]?"

"Huh?" Mr. Paul suddenly stopped his muttering and pounding and looked up at her.

"Sir, I want to go into town and look into procuring us some legitimate transportation to Sulphur Swamp. In addition, I feel a hankering for some new novels and a bag of fresh baby carrot sticks. I find that the vitamin A

---

70. *Foodstuffs, but in fancy-shmancy language.*

and keratin help my apparently inadequate eyesight."

Mr. Paul jumped to his feet and hugged Joan. Staring down at her in disbelief, he exclaimed, "Wait! Hold the presses! You're above deck! Wahoo-wah! And what's this I hear? You want to go into town?"

"Affirmative. Push has come to shove, and I feel it is the appropriate time to partake in drastic action."

Mr. Paul lifted her up in the air. He showered her with kisses. "Yes! Great gadzooks! By all means! Go, go, go! Vamoose! And while you're out, pick up a box of Gorton's fish sticks for me. Okey-dokey, Schmokey-Pokey?"

"Affirmative, Pops."

She stared at him and waited, blank-faced.

Mr. P. put her down and asked, "So? What's wrong?"

"Legal tender. Currency. Moola. I was hoping to avoid the shame-inducing humiliation of begging you for a hand-out, since, at my tender young age, it is illegal for me to engage in legitimate employment, and thus, I am perpetually penniless."

"Oh, oops. Sure. Here." He opened up his wallet and gave her his last twenty-dollar bill. "And don't forget to bring back change, shrimpie-bimpie."

"Affirmative, Mr. Pops." She grabbed Andrew Jackson[71] by the face, leaped off the boat, and onto the dock.

The rickety wooden planks of the dock squeaked and swayed as Joan skipped across their uneven surface towards the shore. As

---

71. *Contrary to popular belief, Andrew Jackson was not a member of the Jackson Five, although Tito Jackson, who many historians claim was the original person chosen to be featured on the twenty dollar bill, was.*

Joan reached the end of the dock, she jumped into the air and landed on the cool, moist earth with a soft, solid shwoomp[72]!

---

72. *Shwoomp is the standard sound effect used for teenage girls landing on soft earth for the first time in eight years.*

CHAPTER FIVE

HAMLET OF SULPHUR SWAMP

After rescuing the baby Redneck, Emmett and Dr. Golem flew straight home to Arkansas. For the next three weeks, the world-famous Sulphur Swamp Language Laboratory of Semiotics, Semantics, and Simians hummed with activity. Their state-of-the-art[73] language experiments with the young chimp were going better than they ever could have expected.

Still, the issue of what to name the

---

73. *The Art, a rotund, beakless green bird that flies backward, is the state bird of Arkansas, so Arkansas is now known as the "State of the Art."*

Redneck remained. Emmett's dad wanted to call him "Diaper Loader," for obvious reasons, but Emmett hated that name. Then, Dr. Golem suggested "Einstein," being as the little guy had already mastered over a hundred words in sign language and was almost ready to begin his Shakespeare lessons. But Emmett didn't like that name, either. Emmett thought the best name was "Taco Breath," because, well, the little Redneck loved tacos and his breath always seemed to smell of them.

In the end, father and son compromised and called him "Hamlet."

Hamlet had a real propensity for sign language, and it was thrilling to watch him learn. He was even inventing new signs of his own. For instance, he would form his hand into a sort of taco-shell shape to signify the word "taco" and put his two fists side by side to signify the word "egg roll." Clearly, most of the words Hamlet invented and used had something to do with food. He was, after all, a growing chimp, and food was very important to him. Yet, Emmett was convinced that soon enough, Hamlet would move beyond food words and write great works of literature, such as MacBeth 2.0, The Sequel.

Mostly, Emmett was thrilled to have a companion. He had never had a real friend before, and he loved it. They spent many hours a day playing slap and tickle[74] as well as other less physical games, like Parcheesi, Frisbee Golf, and Hamlet's personal favorite, Catch My Diaper Before It Hits You Pow In The Head. With Hamlet's taco breath and Emmett's gastritis, they seemed perfectly suited for each other and became instant best friends.

There was, however, one thing that worried Emmett about his new, hairy, little chum: He seemed to suffer from PTSS—post-traumatic stress syndrome. Emmett wasn't a trained therapist, so he couldn't make this diagnosis with complete certainty. However, it was clear to Emmett that Hamlet was emotionally disturbed.

Throughout the day Hamlet seemed happy and well-adjusted, especially for a youngster

---

74. *Get a feather and try it. Fun, fun, fun!*

who had been only recently separated from his parents, ripped out of the jungle, and plopped into Arkansas[75]. But, every night, Emmett would hear Hamlet howling and run to Hamlet's room, only to find the chimp dreaming or, more specifically, nightmaring.

To ease his malaise[76], Emmett would rub Hamlet's belly and sign calming words, like "taco" and "egg roll," until Hamlet's howling subsided. As this continued night after night, Emmett grew more and more worried about his little pal and Hamlet's diapers grew more and more soiled.

Emmett was convinced that Hamlet's howling resulted from nightmares about being separated from his parents, but until

---

75. *Arkansas has some really nice swamps and some good vegetation, but, let's just say, there are not a lot of bananas there for a chimp.*
76. Malaise *is pronounced like mal-aze, and is French for,* Oh, Pierre, that brie gave me a tummy ache!

Emmett's dad finished his DRVDM (Dream Reveal Video Display Machine), there was no way to know sure. And it didn't look like he would ever finish the DRVDM, because, well, ever since they had returned from Africa, his father had seemed severely depressed. And it wasn't the first time Dr. Golem had slipped into a deep funk.

Dr. Melvin Golem had a long history of bouts of severe depression, which is, unfortunately, quite common among geniuses. This stems from the fact that many geniuses have real problems with social interaction. Most people tend to be jealous of geniuses and tease them unmercifully[77]. And then, of course, most geniuses respond by devising extravagant plots to take over the world and exact their revenge. And that inevitably

---

77. *Since I am a genius, as well, I can confirm this hypothesis.*

leads to people labeling them as crazy eccentrics or mad[78] scientists, and once they've been labeled as mad, these scientists feel alienated from society and, inevitably, grow severely depressed. It's a eccentric-genius, mad-scientist, vicious cycle kind of thing.

Emmett was deeply concerned. He had thought his father had overcome his tendency toward depression and that all that mad scientist stuff was in his past.

But obviously, it wasn't. Day after day, his father would wander around the lab in his pajamas and stained, white, terry cloth robe, muttering about semiotics, semantics, and acoustical levitation. He never changed or bathed. He just babbled to himself as he experimented. His nights were spent on the tower's rooftop, right next to the 18-inch

78. *Crazy-mad, not angry-mad, although Melvin was that, too.*

mini-satellite dish he had bought for Emmett, but never bothered to activate. From dusk 'til dawn, he sat on the roof in a folding chair, his feet balanced on the railing and his hands propped behind his head, singing Broadway show tunes as he stared at the stars.

It had gotten so bad that Emmett feared his father might never be able to lift himself out of his funk. If having a successful chimp-language experiment couldn't raise his dad's spirits, what could? Dr. Golem didn't even react to Emmett's gaseous emissions any-more. That was definitely a bad sign.

Dr. Golem's despair continued for the next few weeks. Then, late one night, when Emmett was walking back to his room after a long session of grooming with Hamlet, he heard a noise in his father's lab. Quietly,

Emmett snuck in through the lab's side door.

Emmett quickly hid behind a desk inside the lab. He watched his father take off his terry cloth bathrobe[79] and put on his lab coat. Then, Dr. Golem pointed four hard-plastic conical devices at a ping-pong[80] ball on a table as he muttered, "Acoustical levitation is possible[81]. Yes, yes, yes. If I aim four acoustic transducers emitting ultrasound waves into a central spot, I can create a point of intersection that should suspend objects. Yes, yes, yes! Sound can move mountains! I know it! Ha, ha, ha!"

---

79. *It is de riguer (standard practice) for mad scientists to wear dirty, white, terry cloth bathrobes, but once they take them off, it is usually a good indicator they aren't mad anymore. That is, if they are fully clothed and not naked underneath.*
80. *It is also de riguer to use ping-pong balls for all acoustical levitation scientific experiments.*
81. *The ability to lift objects into the air with sound waves! In scientific circles, this is thought to be impossible and, like time travel, a myth.*

Emmett shook his head sadly and felt deeply wounded. First of all, it's always an ominous sign when a mad scientist laughs hysterically at the end of one of his sentences. Second, everybody knew that acoustical levitation was a myth. No one had ever been able to move objects with sound. Emmett had thought for sure his dad had given up on this dream years before; now it looked like he was obsessed with it again. This did not bode well for the future of the lab, Hamlet, and the whole Golem family.

Emmett had to do something. But what? What can a kid do when his father is obsessed with acoustical levitation?

Countless times, Emmett had heard his father tell the story of the only "supposed" case of successful acoustical levitation. It occurred in the 17th century when a monk by the name of St. Joseph of Cupertino[82] started praying in such a high-pitched, frenzied tone that his body literally rose above the ground, and he soared through the air with a small barnyard animal in his arms.

Emmett was never completely convinced of the St. Joe story and even if it was true, it still had happened over 400 years ago and nobody had levitated since then. Emmett shook his head again and walked dejectedly back to Hamlet's bedroom. Having gastritis was bad, but being obsessed with acoustical levitation was much, much worse. Things were rotten at the world-famous Sulphur Swamp Language Lab. Something had to be done, but what would he do? What could he do?

Emmett turned to Hamlet and conversed

---

82. St. Joseph was known to his friends as "Open Mouth," because he never closed his mouth and, consequently, could never keep a secret.

with him in sign-language. "Dad is mad."

Hamlet answered in sign language, "Taco. Yumm."

Emmett replied, "What should we do about Dad?"

Hamlet answered, "Egg roll. Yumm!"

CHAPTER SIX
TERATOLOGY IN HACKBERRY

A s Joan skipped toward the town of Hackberry, Louisiana, Lazlo Bleak was trudging away from it. He and his flea circus/side-show had set up camp on the edge of this little portside town the day before, and Lazlo had spent the past forty-eight hours looking for potential audience members. He found none, although he did make the acquaintance of several friendly, robust mosquitoes.

Lazlo had returned to camp dispirited. Even though many weeks had passed since the incident in the strange and exotic restaurant in Zimbabwe, Lazlo was still fuming over having his meal ruined by Melvin and Emmett. In addition, he also had a rather large dry-cleaning bill from the blood that had spilt out of his ears onto his nice, new black leather jacket[83].

The first thing Lazlo did once he begrudgingly paid his dry cleaning bill was to drastically alter the Bleak Flea Circus/Side-show World Tour's schedule. Instead of jetting in a luxurious Boeing 747 to all the great cities of Europe, as originally planned, they would tour the most rinky-dink, mediocre[84] cities of the southern United States. And they would do this all in an old Dodge pickup hauling a vintage 1950s, shiny, aluminum-skinned,

---

83. *Dry cleaning leather, especially black leather, is quite pricey.*
84. *Dear citizens of Hackberry, your town is clearly not mediocre, but some of the other towns that Lazlo visited were.*

twenty-six foot trailer[85]—an Airstream Tradewind—which slept six comfortably.

Though Lazlo was known to be a cheap skate, his motivation for rerouting the tour and traveling in a low-budget manner was not merely to save money[86]. In fact, Lazlo planned it as a deliberate attempt to get close to Sulphur Swamp in the most unobtrusive manner possible. In essence, he was determined to wreak utter havoc on Golem and his lab. In doing so, he would get the one thing his heart lusted after most—vengeance, or as Lazlo would say, "Sweeeet, sweeeet revenge!"

Unfortunately for Lazlo, so far, the Southern tour had not been the financial success he had hoped for, which only added to

---

85. *Like a long, thin, silver marshmallow, it was designed for the average American family to hit the road and see America and it was definitely not meant to be used by evil side-show freaks.*
86. *It also allowed him to write off the travel expenses when he did his taxes.*

his unhappiness[87]. Lazlo's cronies didn't seem to mind, though. As a matter of fact, they thought the Southern tour was much more fun than trekking through Europe and/or Africa. And when Lazlo couldn't sell tickets and their shows were cancelled, they were happy to pass the time sunning themselves on top of the Airstream.

But not Lazlo. He hated the sun. Being rather fair-skinned, he worried about skin cancer[88]. So, while his freaks were up on the roof, baking themselves to a crisp, he wandered around looking for people to buy tickets or he sat in the driver's seat of the Dodge Ram-tuff pick-up, counting his money[89].

As he counted, he thought. And when Lazlo

---

87. *He was never really happy, but he liked using his lack of money as an excuse to justify his grouchiness.*
88. *Even if Lazlo is a bad man, we can all learn a lesson from him here and never forget to wear sunblock when we go out.*

thought, he usually came up with something else that made him miserable. And for the past few weeks, ever time he thought, he came to the conclusion that teratology[90] wasn't as much fun or as lucrative as it used to be. With all the recent emphasis on political correctness, there were a lot of places where he couldn't even use the word "freak" in his advertisements. Instead, had to use the term "physically, emotionally, or mentally challenged."

The other troublesome reality was that not many people would pay good money to see physically, emotionally, or mentally challenged people, when, for free, they could see so many freaks on TV and in politics. Plus, the phrase "physically, emotionally, or mentally challenged" was longer than "freak,"

89. *It is de riguer for bad people to spend an inordinate amount of their lives counting their money.*
90. *The study of biological monstrosities, malformations, and malapropisms.*

and since ads were usually billed by the number of letters, it was a lot more expensive to use this more politically correct term. So, Lazlo simply refused to use it.

Lazlo cleared his mind of any and all politically correct thoughts and resumed counting his money. When he finished, he pulled his long, shiny serrated knife out of his thigh holster and grabbed a green apple sitting on the dashboard. He slowly skinned the apple, producing a single, long curly peel.

As he tossed the curly peel out the window, he spotted a pretty young girl wearing large, black cat-eye glasses, ambling along the dirt road toward the Airstream. Lazlo slid the knife back into his thigh holster, got out of the pickup's cab, and checked on his comrades on the roof. Don Juan Frijoles, Marooshka, Bobo, and Fleo didn't even notice the little girl. But Lazlo sure did. Lazlo noticed everything. That's why he was the *de facto*[91] leader. That is why the whole freakish ensemble was called Lazlo Bleak's—and not Fleo's or Bobo's or Marooshka's or The Don's—Flea Circus/Side-show.

Lazlo scampered forward and stood in front of the little girl. Sometimes little girls can be good for a ticket sale, but many times, they are just trouble with a capital T. So, Lazlo was skeptical and decided not to pull any punches.

Lazlo cleared his throat and got right to the point. "Ticketsss are seven-ninety-five, and the next showww doesn't start until sundownnn."

Staring down at the wet earth, Joan meekly trudged up to Lazlo, her hands jammed

---

91. *Latin for* da real.

deeply into her armpits. She hesitated momentarily before inquiring, "Excuse me, kind sir, but it appears as though I am lost."

While Joan had the vocabulary of Noah Webster[92], she also had one of the worst senses of direction in modern history[93]. She had been wandering around the outskirts of Hackberry for hours and had yet to find a market, library, bookstore, or even the center of town[94]. Finally, she had wandered through a bayou and spotted Bleak's rusty old pickup and decrepit Airstream. Owing to Joan's diminutive[95] size, she only noticed a tall, thin-necked man

---

92. *Noah Webster was not the guy who drove the ark; he was the guy who wrote one of the fist dictionaries and, thus, knew a heckuva lot of words.*
93. *Actually, the worst sense of direction in history has to belong to Coonie Snodgrass (1957–1989), who went out for a cup of tea in Bangor, Maine, and ended up in Outer Mongolia seventeen years later, still lost and tea-less.*
94. *Hackberry doesn't really have a town center, but Joan didn't know this.*
95. *A big word that just means small.*

dressed all in black and hadn't notices the naked freaks sunning themselves on the roof.

Bleak stared down at the petite, pigtailed girl and snarled, "I saiddd, would you like to buy a tickettt or nottt, little girlll?"

"*Pardonne moi, monsiuer*[96], I regret to say I am not here to see your highly exploitative, theatrical extravaganza."

"Thennn, what do you wanttt?"

"Ideally, I was yearning for a light literary diversion, and a bag of sweet baby carrot sticks to munch on as I read, and well, Mr. Paul asked for—"

"Noooo, what do you wanttt from meee?"

"I was wondering if you knew, perchance, where the nearest market might be?"

"Do I look like a gasss station attendanttt?"

---

96. *Joan believed that speaking French gave her an air of authority.*

"Negatory, kind sir."

"Turn arounddd and go away, before I am compelleddd to crushhh you into a fine pulppp and use your dusty remains as seasoning for my famousss five-alarm chiliii[97]."

Joan bowed and stepped back nervously. "Um, eh, clearly I have disturbed you. I am deeply sorry, but I desperately need directions. I do not have much legal tender, but what I have, I would graciously split with you if you could offer me succor[98]."

Joan reached down, pulled her father's twenty-dollar bill out of her sock and offered it up to Lazlo. And it was in this pivotal moment that the lives of Joan and Lazlo became forever intertwined, mangled, and connected.

---

97. *Lazlo is not a good man, but, Ooooo, Momma, does he make killer chili.*
98. *Not a lollipop, but, in fact, succor means aid, although, there are times when the perfect form of succor might be a lollipop.*

If only Joan had kept her hands hidden in her armpits like all good little girls are supposed to do. If only she was not so darn innocent. If only she had just listened to Lazlo Bleak and turned around, walked away, and returned to her book-lined sanctuary below deck.

But alas, on this day, for the first time in her thirteen years, Joan had chosen to be brave. She had chosen to go above deck. She had chosen to chat with Lazlo and to offer him money.

And now, she chose not to walk away.

As she held out her cute, stubby, little fingers to Lazlo, he noticed that hiding behind that large, antiquated vocabulary and those retro black cat-eye glasses was a true freak of nature and the perfect addition to his side-show. And in that moment, Lazlo Bleak saw the future of teratology and side-show entertainment.

Yes, in that very moment, Lazlo saw that just below the twenty-dollar bill nestled in Joan's hand were five stunningly gorgeous webbed fingers!

Lazlo was mesmerized. His eyes almost popped out of his skull, his grin spread from ear to ear, and he glowed with excitement. In a suddenly soft, gentle voice, he declared, "Oh, you darlinggg, darlinggg little girl. I'm so sorry. Put your money awayyy. I'd be more than happy to give you directionsss. Now, where oh where did you say you wanted to go?"

Joan smiled and stuck her hands back into her armpits. "Well, kind sir, I was traversing the bayou to find a market for comestibles, more specifically, baby carrot sticks, fish sticks and—"

"Cuttt to the chase, darrrlinggg."

"And once I've purchased a bevy of stick-formed foods, my father and I plan on digesting them as we wait for an idea on how to get our trawler to Hedsuk, Arkansas, home of the Humungo shrimp and Dr. Melvin Golem's world-famous Sulphur Swamp Language Laboratory of Semiotics, Semantics, and Simians."

The eyebrow over Lazlo's left eye twitched[99]. "Excuse me, darlinggg, did you just say, perchance, Melvin Golemmm?"

"Why, yes. Do you know the esteemed doctor?"

"As a matter of facttt, we met a few weeks ago, and I was ssso impressed with his workkk that we were just on our wayyy to pay him a visittt."

"What a fantastic coincidence! Since we do

---

99. *When the left eyebrows of bad guys twitch, head for the hills, baby, because you can rest assured that evil doings are imminent.*

not own a land vehicle and it appears as though you do, would it be possible, perchance, for my father and me to join you on your visit?"

"Why, of course, darlinggg. We would be delighteddd. Go fetch your fatherrr, and as the localsss say, 'Y'all come right back now, ya hearrr.'"

Lazlo offered his long gloved fingers out to Joan. Meekly, she put her tiny webbed paw into his hand, and they shook. As Lazlo touched her, Joan felt a cold, stinging energy flow through her and a sharp pain on both sides of her neck, just beneath her ears. She immediately pulled her hand away and shoved it back into her armpit.

"Um, eh, affirmative, kind sir," Joan said.

She smiled at him and, rubbing her neck, started to walk away. Then, she paused and turned to ask one final question, "Do you surmise that it might be more politic[100] to call Dr. Melvin Golem before visiting? Proper decorum dictates that it is impolite to visit without calling first."

"Don't worry, my darlinggg, I know the good doctor is dyinggg[101] to see meee!"

---

100. *This sounds like politics but really means wise, which most politicians aren't.*
101. *This is a figure of speech, and, in fact, Dr. Golem was not interested in ever seeing Lazlo again, but Lazlo was dying to see Dr. Golem die.*

CHAPTER SEVEN

HUMUNGO SHRIMP COCKTAIL HOUR

Mr. Paul cheered as Lazlo Bleak drove the pickup across the Hedsuk city limits. Joan was sitting in the front seat, sandwiched between Mr. Paul and Lazlo. The ride had been quite pleasant and easy, although there were moments when Lazlo struck Joan as being a bit overwrought.

For example, several times over the course of the drive, Joan noticed that whenever cool zephyrs blew in through the pickup's window, Lazlo would jump and mumble, "Momma, nooo, pleassse."

Then, as day turned to night and they drove across sections of the highway in which tall, leafy trees hung down low below the streetlights, causing an eerie blue-white shadowy glow to reflect onto the pickup's windshield, Lazlo would murmur, "I'lll beee a good boyyy, Momma, I will, I promise!"

Joan looked up at the barrel-chested man in black sitting next to her, his greasy pompadour sliding up against the hard metal interior of the driver's cab.

Trying not to be intrusive, Joan quietly asked him, "Excuse me, kind sir, but I couldn't help overhearing you mention your mother every time we are struck by a bone-chilling breeze or an uncanny shadow—"

Lazlo barked at her, "It's nothinggg! Nothinggg! My mother was a fine, upstandinggg citizennn. Not a thievinggg, curseslinginggg, gypsy fortunetellerrr!"

Joan considered pursuing the topic farther, but she noticed how his entire body had tensed up and all the veins in his forehead seemed to be bursting through his skin when she had mentioned his mother. So, she refrained, thinking it best to respect his privacy. But clearly, Lazlo was a bit jumpy, especially at night, and he suffered from deep-seated mother issues. Joan wished she had her old fish stick-shaped nightlight[102] with her, so she could give it to him. She knew how comforting it had been to her when she used to get scared of the dark.

Yet, Lazlo did have his own version of a fish stick-shaped nightlight. He combatted his nighttime heebie-jeebies by playing a homemade

---

102. *Besides inventing fish sticks, Mr. P. also invented a fish stick-shaped nightlight just for Joan, which always made her feel safe in the dark.*

cassette tape of the entire collected master-works of the disco[103] era, over and over again, throughout the whole nine-hour trip. Of course, there were times when Joan wanted to ask for a bit of musical variation, maybe some bluegrass, polka tunes, or even a little Zydeco[104], but she thought it impolite to say so. In the end, it really didn't matter, since during the whole ride, she had been suffering such severe neck pain that she really couldn't enjoy the music, anyhow.

But Mr. Paul loved every one of the disco tunes, especially "I Will Survive." He sang along with the music, and, in fact, during "It's Raining Men," he thought he heard voic-es coming from the Airstream, singing along

---

103. *Lazlo considered disco to be the sacred music of freaks and geeks.*

104. *Zydeco is the rock 'n roll of the bayou, and one of the best things about it is that many of the instruments used in this style of music can also be used to clean clothing.*

with him. Mr. P. assumed it was some type of echo. He and Joan had no idea that four disco-loving, but mean-spirited and evil-hearted, mutants of nature were riding in the trailer only a few feet behind him.

Joan glanced over at her father. She had never seen Mr. Paul in such a state. He was downright giddy. Sure, the disco music was upbeat, but it was definitely more than that. Joan suspected that the mere thought of all those Humungo shrimp was making Mr. P. radiate with joy.

Personally, Joan didn't care much for shrimp farming, but knowing that her father's dream was finally coming true made her the happiest little girl in all of Arkansas. She had been above deck almost thirteen hours now, and everything seemed to be working out really well. Her father's plan was finally coming to fruition, and for the first time in many years, she wasn't worried about a single thing.

But she should have been. She should have been more worried than she'd ever been in her entire worrisome, below-deck life. She should have been worried sick about not sticking to her plan. She should have been terribly worried about not returning immediately to her little sanctuary below deck. She should have been horribly worried about dragging her father away from the safety of the trawler and into the clutches of one evil, pencil-neck geek named Lazlo Bleak.

She should have been worried to death about all these things, because in several recent significant polls, the flea circus ringmaster and pencil-neck geek she was now sitting next to had been rated as one of the top five most ruthless, shrewd, and evil people in the entire world.

In fact, Lazlo was so ruthless, shrewd, and evil, he had NOT read just one article in *Small Trawler Fisherman Monthly*; before embarking on his southern tour, he had read every single book, magazine article, internet posting, and random piece of information in existence relating to Hedsuk, Humungo shrimp, Sulphur Swamp, and Dr. Melvin Golem. As a result, Lazlo knew a great deal more about the dangers associated with Humungos[105] than Joan or her father, but since he was so ruthless, shrewd, and evil, he kept all that knowledge to himself.

Lazlo drove by a huge neon sign that read: Sulphur Swamp Language Laboratory of Semiotics, Semantics, and Simians, 1/4 Mile.

---

105. *You'll see. Those cute Humungos are more than just mighty good eating.*

Mr. P. literally bopped up and down in his seat with excitement. They were so close. So close!

But a mile later, Lazlo still had not turned off the road toward the lab. Mr. P. was fidgeting and looking around nervously. He didn't want to be rude, but they had clearly missed the turn and he was visibly upset.

Deciding to speak up on her father's behalf, Joan leaned toward Lazlo, cleared her throat, and inquired, "Um, excuse me, kind sir, but I think we passed the lab a mile back."

"Why, yes, darlinggg. We diddd."

"My father and I were of the belief that it would be judicious to stop there before we went to Sulphur Swamp."

"Of course, the labbb would be a good place to visittt, but we came for the Humungo shrimpppp, didn't we, Mr. Paulll?"

Mr. Paul screamed, "Yeah, baby, yeah!"

"So, I thought it would be more fun to stoppp at the Sulphur Swamp docksss firsttt and see a Humungo shrimppp or two before we wenttt to the labbb. Scientific labsss can be sooo dreary."

Mr. Paul chimed in, "Fantastic! Humungos, here we come!"

They drove on for a hundred more feet before they saw another sign that read: *Sulphur Swamp. 1/4 Mile. Turn Right at Stop Sign at Sisyphus Circle*[106].

A quarter-mile later, they ran into the stop sign at the corner of Sisyphus Circle and the interstate... Literally. The Dodge pickup crashed into the sign, cracking its post in half. Lazlo was so evil, he didn't even care. He just backed away from the broken sign,

---

106. *Sisyphus Circle is a funny street, because every time you try to get to the end of it, you always find yourself back at the beginning.*

turned the wheel to the right, and drove down Sisyphus Circle.

As the pickup and Airstream trailer rolled toward the swamp, the first thing that struck Joan was the horrendous sulphur stench. This was not your average, stink bomb-caliber odor. This was a grab-your-nose-bend-over-and-barf-caliber stink. Imagine a crate of cracked eggs, open and rotting in the sun for weeks on end. Then, imagine building a chicken coop over that and installing a few thousand dead chickens. Then, imagine dumping the dead carcasses of a few thousand tuna on top of them. Then, imagine covering it all in elephant dung. And it doesn't even come close to one-tenth of the vile horrendousness of the stench emanating from Sulphur Swamp.

But all Mr. Paul smelled was the sweet

green scent of money. Joan, on the other hand, almost passed out. As she started to topple, Lazlo reached over and steadied her. Covering her mouth and nose with her hand, she forced herself to sit up straight. Groans and gags came from the back of the Airstream, but Joan was so absorbed in trying not to be overcome by the odor that she didn't even hear them. Even Lazlo was affected. As he parked the pickup next to a rickety, old wooden dock, he coughed and covered his mouth and nose with his hanky.

Joan looked out toward the brown water of the swamp. At first, all she could see was a dense, foggy marine layer. But even without a clear view of the swamp and its inhabitants, she knew they had found the Humungos. She had read about their weird, high-pitched, yelping shellfish twitter and she instantly recognized the clamorous din.

As awful as the stench of Sulphur Swamp was, it was nothing compared to the strange, deafening racket of millions of Hedsuk Humungo shrimps roughhousing underwater, not to mention on the surface of the water and even in the air above the water. Gigantic ten-pounders were flying through the air and jumping onto each other. Baby Humungos were crawling around the sand and searching for their parents. It was a Humungo shrimpapalooza, and it had to be the single strangest thing Joan had ever seen[107].

Mr. Paul jumped out of the cab of the pick-up. He was in crustacean heaven[108]. At the shore of the swamp, Mr. P. fell to his knees, raised his hands to the skies, and cried, "Watch out, world, Mr. P. is back! I've found my own little slice of paradise and I'm gonna be rich! Rich! RICH!"

And then, Mr. P. rose back onto his feet, spread his arms out wide, and started to sing, "Money! Money! Money![109]"

After finishing his little ditty, Mr. P. start-ed chasing Humungo shrimp around the empty dock area. Joanie watched him, laugh-

---

107. *True, if someone remains below deck for her whole life, she may not see a lot, but Joan did spend a lot of time looking out the porthole window, and, either way, she had never read about anything like this.*
108. *The place where all good, crusty, batter seafood go after they are eaten.*
109. *It is* de riguer *for people who think they are about to become instant millionaires to sing the praises of money.*

ing at first and then coughing from inhaling so much of the sulphur stench.

Lazlo handed Joan his white handkerchief. She took it from him, graciously nodded her thanks, and slowly covered her nose and mouth. Lazlo did the same with his gloved hand. Then, he exited the cab of the pickup. He held his left hand out to her and assisted Joan as she stepped from the vehicle. They both marched toward the swamp.

As they walked, Joan tugged on Lazlo's sleeve and then said, "Dear kind sir, why do you think no other shrimpers are here farming these Humungo shrimp?"

"Who knowsss? It isss quite late in the eveninggg, and maybe it isss not Humungo shrimppp season yettt?"

Still, it was unusual. So many shrimp and so few shrimpers. Something was fishy here in Sulphur Swamp.

After that article in *Small Trawler Fisherman Monthly*, Joan had assumed Sulphur Swamp would be swarming with fisherman, but the place was completely deserted. For the first time in hours, Joan was starting to worry.

She was concerned that she really should have done more research. It was so unlike her to just blindly follow her father. She worried that she should have read more about Sulphur Swamp, about Humungo shrimp, and even about the swamps of Arkansas. She bemoaned the fact that her trawler library was so limited. All her books dealt with trivial things, like love, art, and death, while not a single one dealt with shrimping.

Without a background of research to pull from, Joan had to draw her own conclusions.

Joan reasoned that Sulphur Swamp must be deserted because it was nighttime and most shrimpers work in the morning. In addition, Sulphur Swamp was clearly quite hard to locate, and of course, the smell could keep away all but the heartiest souls.

Still, something disturbed Joan. The swamp just seemed too devoid of human activity. As much as she tried not to, she felt haunted by bad feelings. The sides of her throat felt hot and throbbed painfully. And when she wiped her hands against her painfully pulsing neck, there were a few droplets of blood on her fingertips.

Something was definitely terribly wrong. But before she could say anything, Joan was made breathless by one of the most horrifically grotesque incidents in modern history.

Mr. Paul, in his naïve, child-like exuberance, had chased a pair of Humungo shrimp into the swamp. Suddenly, as Mr. P. splashed about in the murky waters, he let out a blood-curdling scream. At first, Joan assumed that he was simply upset about getting his new boots wet or that the water was irritating his flesh. Either of those alternatives would have been a blessing compared to the grotesque reality of Mr. P.'s predicament.

It was the Humungo shrimp. They were not vegans[110] like most shrimp; indeed, Humungos were carnivores[111], and Mr. P., the fish stick and tartar sauce king of Love Canal, was their early bird special. Dinner was being served at Sulphur Swamp, and the main course was live, bearded, yellow-slick-ered fisherman.

---

110. *Creatures who don't eat meat and won't wear leather handbags.*
111. *Carnivores like meat, especially meat at carnivals, like corn dogs.*

Oh, the soulless, diabolical treachery of those horrid Humungos! And oh, the soulless, diabolical treachery of Lazlo for bringing Joan and Mr. P. to this fetid, treacherous place, knowing full well what would happen when Mr. Paul saw all those shrimp.

Joan screamed, "Nooo, Pops!"

She tried to dash into the water to rescue him, but Lazlo held her back.

"Don't, my darlinggg," he snarled. "There's nothinggg you can do—"

"But—"

"You musn'ttt, or they'll get you, too."

Joan struggled against Lazlo's grip, but he held onto her firmly. If only she was closer, she might have been able to do something to save her beloved father, but alas, she was too far away to do anything but watch in utter horror[112].

At first, Joan thought Mr. P. was squirting blood everywhere. That is, until she saw him reach down, stick his index finger in a pool of the thick red fluid, lick his finger clean, and exclaim, "Hmm... Tastes like cocktail sauce."

Yes, the Humungos were squirting gallons of a horseradishy secretion of cocktail sauce onto Mr. Paul. Joan stared at him, but before she could say anything, he yelled to her, "Mmmm-mmmm, horseradishy-good! I'm okay, Joan. No worries."

But Joan did have worries. Big worries. Humongo worries. For she suddenly realized what was really happening. The Humungos were spraying a red, horseradishy secretion onto him as merely a sort of pre-meal ritual

---

112. *If you have recently eaten a large meal or are already feeling a bit under the weather, it is probably best for you to skip the next few pages or at least grab a barf bag now, while you have the time and ability.*

before tearing away at his flesh. "Noooo!" she screamed to her father. "Get out of the water! Now!"

But Mr. Paul didn't seem to hear her. In fact, he didn't even seem to realize what the Humungos were up to...

A slight smile seemed to creep across Lazlo's lips as he witnessed the giant shrimpies preparing for the massacre. Yet, when Joan glanced over at him, he quickly took on the traditional innocent bystander look of horror and urged, in a not-so-convincing manner, "Run, Mr. P. Quickkk. Runnn."

Mr. P. finally caught on to what was happening to him. But at this point, even though he tried to fight the frenzied hordes of Humungos, it was too late. The shrimp were blanketing him in a spicy cocktail sauce that burned his skin raw. Joan desperately wanted to save her dad, but she could think of nothing to do that wouldn't also jeopardize her own life.

Then, suddenly, a miracle seemed to occur. All the Humungos dispersed and swam away from Mr. Paul. He was going to survive. Sure, his skin would be raw for awhile, but they had given him a reprieve and he would be okay. Overjoyed, Joan screamed, "Tis over. He's alive... Thank God."

She jumped up and down with happiness. Mr. P. hobbled toward her on the shore, but he was only able to take a few steps before a blood-curdling moan lanced the foggy air. Something was rising from the swamp's pungent depths.

The swamp water parted amid swirling foam as the Queen Humungo emerged from the depths, wearing a glittery, green, kelpy, seaweedy gown. With her massive size, slimy garb, bulging eyes, and razor-sharp, beeky jaw that kept clamping open and shut, she was a truly horrifying sight. In her bristly clawed appendages, she held something large, ominous, and yellow.

A lemon. A huge, yellow lemon.

As Mr. Paul stared at her, frozen in horror, the Queen Humungo grabbed him in one of her barnacled claws, ripped the lemon in two with her other claw, and squirted each half of the fruit into Mr. P.'s eyes. Mr. Paul screamed in pain, as he was completely blinded by the acidic fluid. Then, the Queen bent over and bit a huge chunk out of his skull.

What happened next was truly grotesque. Joan covered

her eyes as thousands of Humungo attached themselves to every part of his body and ate in a frenzy of blood and gore. Horrible gobbling and munching sounds filled the air as the sun set over Sulphur Swamp.

As he watched Mr. Paul's gory demise, Lazlo thought of telling Joan the truth. Sulphur Swamp was empty of human activity because it is common knowledge among anyone who has ever read anything other than just *Small Trawler Fisherman Monthly*[113] that Humungo shrimp are more deadly than piranhas or barracudas[114]. But then, because Lazlo didn't want to lose his status as one of

---

113. *Not to denigrate this fine magazine, but educated people know that one ought to refer to more than a single source for reliable information.*
114. *After extensive research and cajoling, I was able to force Dr. Melvin Golem to admit to me that he spliced some piranha and barracuda DNA into the Humungo shrimp DNA. He never considered the ramifications, and that, my dear friends, is the reality of science without boundaries!*

the most ruthless, shrewd, and evil people in the world, he decided not to tell her anything.

As the feeding frenzy died out, Joan buried her head in Lazlo's leather jacket and cried and cried and cried.

"We should have stopped him. It's our fault," she said.

"No, darlinggg. There's nothing we could have done. It's over nowww. Come, let me fixxx you a cuppp of tea."

Lazlo led a devastated Joan away from the swamp and into the back of the Airstream. As she entered, she was so distraught that she didn't even notice the shadows of the four people hiding among the furniture in the trailer. She just sat down in a little chair next to a small cage in the middle of the trailer.

Lazlo gave her a cup of hot tea that he poured out of a thermos. Joan took the tea and held the warm cup between her cold palms. She took a long sip and tried to ignore her neck pain. She was still crying. She just couldn't get the image of her father's grotesque death out of her mind. Her neck pulsed painfully now, and she just wanted to go home.

Lazlo stroked her little head and said, "Why don't you take off your shoesss and relaxxx? You've been through sooooo much todayyy."

She put down her cup, untied her shoes, and removed them.

"Take your socksss offf, too."

Normally, Joan wouldn't have complied so readily, since she was always bashful about her webbed appendages, but she was so stunned by her father's death that she just followed Lazlo's orders blindly. As she yanked

off her socks, Lazlo stared in
wonder.

Yes, just as he suspected:
She had webbed feet,
too. Lazlo smiled,
knowing she would be
a fantastic addition to the side-show.

Joan spoke up, "Kind sir, I would be most
appreciative if you would please take me
back to my trawler."

"Why, of course. But I think that, firsttt, we
need to stoppp at the Labbb and reporttt this
unfortunate incidenttt to the police, don't you
agree?"

"Affirmative. You are right, kind sir."

"Put your shoesss back on and come up to
the fronttt seat with meee. We should go
nowww."

Joan put on her socks and shoes. She

wiped her nose and her eyes.

"May I take this tea with me?" she asked.

"Of course," Lazlo answered.

She took her cup of tea and followed Lazlo out of the back of the Airstream.

This had to be the single worst day of her life. Depressed and convinced her life was over, she plopped back down into the front seat of the pickup next to Lazlo. He immediately flicked on the cassette player, filling the cab with the upbeat disco tempo of "Disco Duck."

Joan was an orphan again. She felt sad, confused, lost, and alone. But she was also comforted by the fact that she had met this kind man who seemed to care deeply about her.

She felt confident Lazlo would help take care of her. He would bring her to the Lab and then back to her trawler, and she would stay below deck for the rest of her life and try to forget about this horrible day.

How fortunate she was to have stumbled into Lazlo Bleak on the outskirts of Hackberry. How fortunate that he was now going to escort her safely back to her sanctuary below deck.

Or so she thought.

CHAPTER EIGHT

THE SWITCHBACK OF DEATH

Throughout U.S. history, great Americans like Benjamin Franklin, Abraham Lincoln, and Joan Paul have all valued two related ideas above all others: independence and autonomy[115]. Emerging from poverty-stricken backgrounds and being largely self-taught, all three of these influential thinkers were uncomfortable with relying on others. Eventually, though, despite their considerable autonomy, they all had to reach out to and depend upon others. In the

---

115. *Autonomy is like independence, but better.*

cases of Franklin and Lincoln, much of their success and happiness in life stemmed from their keen, intuitive ability to pick the right people to trust and depend on.

Young Joan, on the other hand, had no idea how to choose whom to trust. For the first thirteen years of her life, the only non-fictional person she had ever really spent time with was Mr. Paul, and he had always proven to be kind and trustworthy. So, after his grisly demise, Joan naturally assumed that since Lazlo was approximately the same age and height[116] as her father, he would prove to be similarly trustworthy.

Unfortunately, trusting a certain pencil-neck geek by the name of Lazlo Bleak was absolutely the wrong choice. After all, Lazlo

---

116. *Further proof that young people should not trust adults simply because they have achieved a certain age or height.*

happened to be, according to several significant recent polls, one of the top five most untrustworthy people in the world.

It is worth noting that trusting Lazlo was not her first big mistake; it was, in fact, her second. Her first huge mistake was her foolish decision to depart her sanctuary below deck. Many people can spend their entire lives below deck and be very happy. Joan ignored this fact and chose to try new things, to try to grow as a young woman and a human being, and that is exactly what had caused her so many problems.

Of course, Joan was also still grieving deeply for her dearly departed father. Though she tried to hold back her tears, she couldn't stop herself from sobbing quietly while she rested her head against Lazlo's cold shoulder.

As night fell over the town of Hedsuk, ominous clouds blanketed the sky. The moon tried to poke its face through the pea-soupy storm clouds, but they were just too thick. Even though it was still early in the evening, the streets of Hedsuk were quiet. It appeared as though thundershowers were heading into town and not ordinary t-storms, but hurricane-caliber storms.

Lazlo didn't care about the weather; he had bigger fish to fry[117]. As soon as he spotted the sign for the lab, he turned left and drove onto the lab's private road. The lab was more than a mile off the main road and most of that mile went straight up at a sharp incline. In fact, the lab was situated upon the apex of a sheer cliff known as Mt. Hedsuk, which overlooked

---

117. *He actually hated fried fish, but this is a commonly used expression that sounds funny if it is altered to something like, "Bigger foxes to fry."*

all of Sulphur Swamp.

Lazlo downshifted as he began the precarious journey up Mt. Hedsuk. The lab's private dirt road needed major repairs and was filled with cracks, crevices, and boulders. As Lazlo shifted, the Dodge pickup bounced in and out of a rut, lurching forward and tossing Joan up into the air. She landed back in her seat hard, all the while, not allowing herself to cry, even though she wanted to very badly. She wiped her nose with her sleeve[118], cleaned her glasses with her shirt, and stared up at the shimmering steel-and-glass lab on the top of the mountain.

Suddenly, the clouds above them burst open, releasing a torrent of rain that hammered the roof of the pickup and the Airstream with large, heavy water pellets. It

---

118. *Clearly, no tissues were available.*

sounded like they were passing through a driving range and being pelted with golf balls. Lazlo rolled up his window and drove on.

The lab's private, circuitous, dirt road wound its way up the mountain, twisting back and forth for more than a mile before ending suddenly at the lab's front door. As the rain fell, the road grew slick and muddy, but Lazlo did not slow down. In fact, he just stepped harder on the accelerator and sped forward.

Mt. Hedsuck was a huge quartz and granite rock formation. The higher the mountain rose, the less vegetation covered it. As they drove toward the peak, Joan glanced down at Sulphur Swamp below. Through the pouring rain, she thought she could see the faint outlines of Humungos frolicking about, energized by their recent feast. She quickly pulled her gaze away and covered her eyes.

The pickup bucked and strained as it plowed its way up the steep grade. Every time the vehicle reached a sharp turn on the serpentine road, Joan felt the wheels lose their grip, and she was sure they were going to slip in the mud, fly over the edge, and fall hundreds of feet into the deadly swamp. Yet, somehow, Lazlo managed to steer the vehicle back on course each time.

Finally, twelve minutes after they'd started up the dirt road, the pickup ground to a halt at the iron front gates of the Sulphur Swamp Language Lab of Semantics, Semiotics, and Simians. From her seat, Joan could see the monolithic, circular building with its pointed, gothic, cathedral-like tower emerging out of the center of the structure and rising all the way up to the clouds. Like a huge steel and glass bagel with a tremendous can of whipped cream[119] rising from its center, the lab was a bizarre sight. Amid the darkness, it glowed and hummed with an eerie fluorescent light.

Lazlo lowered his window, reached out into the rain, poked the red intercom button on the front gate, and announced, "Yes, hello, this is Dr. Smith and my colleagues from the American Association of Semantics, Semiotics, and Simians. We are here for our annual surprise inspection."

A second later, a cracking high-pitched voice echoed out of the intercom system, "Um, eh... Wait a second.... We didn't know about any—"

"That is why it is called a surprise inspection–"

---

119. *Many scholars now believe that Golem's tower actually served as the inspiration for the first can of mass-produced whipped cream.*

"Oh.... Dad, some people are here for an inspection. ... Alright. ... You sure? ... Okay. Yes, come in, please."

Joan looked up at Lazlo as he drove though the gate and onto the circular paved black asphalt driveway that swept along the front edge of the laboratory complex. The plants and trees around the lab looked wild and untended. Up close, the lab appeared worn and shabby. The glass walls were filthy and begging for a good scrubbing. Even the buckets of rain that were pouring down upon the lab seemed incapable of washing away the dark grime that had accumulated on the walls over the years.

Joan looked at Lazlo and said, "Excuse me, kind sir, but, number one, I thought we were here to report my father's demise, and number two, I was also under the assumption that you were employed exclusively in show business?"

Lazlo answered, "Well, yesss, we will call about your fatherrr, and I am in show businesss, but like many show people, to make a little extra income[120], I do some odd jobsss, such as laboratory inspectionsss."

"Yet, your name is not Smith, affirmative?"

"Affirmative. My inspectionsss must be a surprissse, and so, I alwayssss do them incognito[121], under the psuedonym, Dr. Smith. Clever, eh?"

"Very," Joan nodded.

Lazlo pointed to an old brown clipboard on the top of the dashboard. "Dear childdd, can

---

120. *In Lazlo's defense, most people in the flea circus/side-show business these days do have a second job to help support themselves. This is merely a function of the fact that exhibiting freaks just doesn't pay as well as it used to, especially when freaks are so readily viewable in 7-11's, the Gap, and Laundromats across the country.*

121. *In most cases, if someone you are with claims to be doing something incognito, it is fair to assume they are up to no good, not good at all!*

you please handddd me that clipboarddd?"

Joan handed him the clipboard as he parked the pickup in front of the dual sliding glass door entrance to the lab. Joan heard a loud, creaking noise as the back door of the Airstream swung open and four rather extraordinary-looking mutants emerged alongside the front of the vehicle.

Joan asked, "Ergo, thus, and hence, those must be your trusted colleagues and fellow inspectors. Affirmative?"

"Affirmative, dear girlll."

Lazlo pocketed his keys, tapped his large knife to make sure it was in place securely along his thigh, and pulled a huge handful of ultrasonic earplugs[122] out of his pocket. He

---

122. *Lazlo, like the Boy Scouts who awarded him the Eagle Scout badge when he was a mere stripling, had vowed to "be prepared," and so, he pre-ordered earplugs, knowing one day he would again be in close proximity to Emmett and Melvin Golem.*

placed two in his ears and jumped out of the pickup. Lazlo then grabbed an umbrella out from underneath his seat and opened it. Once the umbrella was opened and poised over the passenger door to the pickup, he guided Joan out, making sure she did not get even a droplet of rain on her.

Lazlo's four colleagues followed behind him and Joan as they sauntered over to the lab's front door. Lazlo distributed earplugs to each of his colleagues, who took the plugs and inserted them into their ears. Everyone stood erect in the pouring rain, except for Joan, who was now holding Lazlo's umbrella. Though Joan remained dry, she shivered from the cold.

"Here, darlinggg," Lazlo said, as he handed Joan a pair of ear plugs. "Many timesss, these language lab-sss can get very loud. Safety firsttt, affirmative?"

"Affirmative, kind sir." Joan smiled and put the plugs into her ears.

She was still sad, of course, but this sweet man in black seemed to be deeply concerned with helping her maintain her limited, but adequate auditory[123] powers.

Lazlo signaled to the four mutants, and they all stepped to the side. Then, he whispered to Joan, "Dearrr girl, you may go firsttt and make your phone call. It will help maintain the element of surprissse, so essential to life as a surprissse inspector."

"Why, of course. Maybe they might even have a spot of tea or cocoa to offer?"

As Joan walked toward the front of the complex, the rain subsided[124] as suddenly as it had started. So, Joan stopped, folded up the umbrella, politely handed it back to Lazlo, and turned back to the door, trying not to slip on the slick asphalt.

A strong, earthy aroma filled the air as

---

123. *Of and/or relating to hearing and the ears, as well as earwax.*
124. *A fancy, scientific way to say* stop, *especially in the name of love.*

Joan approached the large glass sliding doors. She was eager to report her father's death to the police and did not pay much attention to what Lazlo and his friends were up to. But if she did, she would have noticed that they did not follow close behind her. Instead, they had pulled away from her and remained about thirty feet behind, tucked away next to some shrubbery.

Joan reached out and tried to knock on the slick glass door, but before she could, it slid open with a squeaky, painful groan. As she stuck her head inside the lab, she smelled something strange. It was a cold, sterile scent mixed with the earthy, funky jungle smell of an animal, or to be more exact, a chimp.

Joan hoped and prayed that maybe, just maybe this was the smell of salvation and that her troubles would finally be over. But she was wrong, dead wrong...

CHAPTER NINE

LAZLO'S LANGUAGE LAB OF HORRORS

Science is a strange thing and, at times, quite grotesque in a paradoxical[125] sort of way. The trouble with science is simply that what one person may think of as a true, verifiable scientific fact, another person may think of as complete hogwash[126].

But science is responsible for much of the good in our lives, such as anti-mole sonar

---

125. *A paradox is a couple of ducks, usually a male and female mallard, and can also be a mysterious riddle.*
126. *Hogwash is not a pretty sight. Especially on hot days when the wash coming off of hogs is filled with a putrid, piggy stench.*

sticks, Teflon-coated waffle-makers, sugar-less sugar-substitutes, and Wow Potato Chips with Olean[127]. And it was science that brought Joan and Emmett together. Or, more specifically, it was a scientifically designed automatic glass door that scanned Emmett's retina, slid open, and allowed Joan and Emmett to finally meet.

When Joan stepped into the lab and laid eyes upon Emmett, the first thing she noticed about him was that a Redneck chimp was hanging from his neck. A moment later, Dr. Golem, still straightening up his white, terry cloth bathrobe, appeared right behind Emmett. As they stared at her, a nervous Joan tucked her hands under her armpits.

In the cold, white-walled lab lobby, Joan took a single step forward and stood facing

---

127. *A soybean-based fat substitute that causes anal leakage.*

Emmett, his father, and their Redneck. She tried to appear friendly and rocked back and forth from her toes to her heels as she spoke, "Um, eh, greetings. My name is Joan Paul. So sorry to inconvenience you at such a late hour, but, you see, a terrible accident has happened to my father in the swamp below, and thus, ergo, and hence, I was wondering if I could use your phone to alert the authorities while the surprise inspectors do their job?"

As she spoke, Joan looked down at the ground, but then, realizing how rude that was, she forced herself to look back up. Her green eyes met Emmett's soft, blue eyes. Emmett found himself drawn to her, as if he knew her.

For a moment, he was frozen, speechless. He nervously tapped his foot against the ground and his hand against his thigh. Then, he waved at her and said, "Hi."

Hamlet, too, signed the word for "Hi."

Joan answered, "Greetings. I have read several noted books on Ameslan, and thus, hence, and ergo, if my memory serves me correctly, I believe that your young Redneck just said hello to me as well."

Emmett stared in disbelief. A weird, brainy young girl had stepped into his life. He was thrilled, yet, at the same time, a nervous wreck. He wanted to say the right thing, to make the correct first impression. But as he looked at her and fumbled for words, all the circuits in his brain seemed to criss-cross and short-circuit. Try as he might to look calm, cool, and collected, his limbs betrayed him. His feet tapped furiously against the ground, and his hands shook.

Then, all of sudden, words started popping

out of his mouth like watermelon seeds. "Yep. Um... Like, um, dude, why do you talk like, you know, that?"

Emmett couldn't believe what he'd just said. He was such a jerk! He knew that if only he had been able to go to school and had more experience with girls, he would have been able to handle this situation so much better.

But before he could apologize, Joan asked, "Excuse me? It is mean-spirited to denigrate[128] the way I talk when your voice fluctuates between being irritatingly high-pitched to scathingly low-pitched."

"Um, like, I have no clue what you just said, but, like, dude, where'd you get those glasses? Because, like, um, you know, nobody wears glasses like that anymore."

"They were a gift from my fa... Fa...

_____

128. *A fancy word that means to put someone down.*

Father."

And then, Joan started to weep. Loudly and profusely.

Emmett felt horrible. Was it inappropriate to call girls, "Dude"? He had no idea what he had said that could have made her cry. Admittedly, he had been a bit curt[129], and he probably shouldn't have made fun of her glasses, but having never really spoken to someone close to his age, especially a cute young teenage girl, he was ill-prepared for urbane conversation[130]. And when he was nervous, he tended to overtalk and say the first thing that popped into his head, which was usually something stupid.

Dr. Golem flicked Emmett's earlobe with his index finger

and said, "Be nice. Where are your man-ners?"

"Dad!" Emmett yelled.

Dr. Golem shook Joan's hand and said, "Sorry about my son. He doesn't get out much.... Here, here, don't cry. Everything's gonna be okay."

Then, putting his arm around Joan, Dr. Golem said, "Please come into the kitchen, and I'll make you some hot cocoa." He took a step toward the kitchen and then paused to ask, "I must say, I'm a bit confused. Could you tell me again, who you are, and why you are here?"

Joan, Emmett, and Dr. Golem took a few steps in sync through the long lobby toward

---

129. *Emmett's name was, obviously, Emmett, and not Curt, but to be curt does not mean to be named Curt; it means to be abrupt and not very loquacious.*
130. *Urbane conversation usually involves references to cultural things, like hoity-toity museums, literature, and cucumber finger sandwiches, and does not refer to urban music, which is a nice way of saying music from inner-city people of color.*

the kitchen. In between sobs, Joan said, "My name is Joan Paul. I'm here to make a phone call to the police to report my father's accidental death as a result of a Humungo shrimp attack. And the lab inspectors I'm here with were gracious enough to provide me with transportation."

"Oh, yes, the inspectors. And where are they?"

"Well, a second ago, they were right behind me."

As a glowing full moon popped out from beneath a cloud, Lazlo waltzed into the entranceway of the lobby. His followers moved in right behind him, dripping water all over the floor, since they hadn't even bothered to wipe their feet[131].

Emmett stared at the grotesque gang standing in front of him in the foyer.[132] Instinctively, he backed away from them and swung his body in front of Hamlet. As he did so, Dr. Golem smiled, offered his hand to Lazlo, and said, "Welcome, Dr. Smith—"

Emmett hollered at him, "Dad, Gawwwd! He's not Dr. Smith! They're the flesh-eating psychos from Africa. They want to kill Hamlet—"

Lazlo's face filled with a large grin, and he said, "Actually, we wanttt to killl all of you. Although, I think the chimppp is the only one that we shalll eattt, being as you and your fatherrr do not lookkk very appetizinggg."

Joan was stunned. What was going on? What were they talking about? Her neck tensed with a pulsing pain. She pulled away from Dr. Golem, grabbed her throat, and started to weep again. This had to be the

131. *Not wiping one's feet is a sure sign of an evil heart.*
132. *A fancy word for the front of a lobby which is pronounced four-yay, even though it is not spelled that way. Many would argue it is a result of the French.*

worst day of her whole life. First, her father's death, and now this.

Joan opened her mouth to speak, but before she had a chance to say anything, Lazlo snapped his fingers, and his four mutant inspectors exploded into action. The Don's tail whipped around, whacking Dr. Golem's legs out from underneath him. This sent him flying to the floor where he smashed his head on the hard concrete and was knocked out cold.

A second later, with a loud "Sephalapagoo Kazooo![133]" Fleo sent her phalanx[134] of fleas flying at Emmett and Hamlet. They formed a large blurry arrow and dove in for the kill. Hamlet started howling in fear and jumped onto

---

133. One of Fleo's standard flea commands, which roughly translated into English means, "Go, fly fast, you crazy little parasites-for-sore-eyes."
134. Like a platoon, but sounds better, because ph sounds like f, which alliterates well with the word fleas.

the chandelier in the front hallway. Emmett screamed so loud, the power of his outburst sent the fleas bouncing back to their owner[135].

Meanwhile, Lazlo slapped Bobo and sent him bouncing toward the chandelier. Hamlet screeched, swinging off the chandelier and taking off down the circular hallway toward the labs, with Bobo hot on his tail, bouncing after him.

135. *Unfortunately for Fleo's fleas, Lazlo had not taken the time to hand them mini-ultrasonic earplugs.*

Marooshka jumped over the unconscious doctor and cracked her bullwhip at Emmett. The hard leather snapped against his chest, tearing his shirt, but surprisingly, drawing no blood.

Emmett started yelling louder, and his high-pitched shriek shattered a large mirror in the hallway. Yet, much to Emmett's surprise, the mirror seemed to be the only thing affected by his vocal assault. Clearly, the ultrasonic earplugs that Lazlo and his gang had shoved in their ears were working their magic.

Emmett took off after Hamlet.

"Freeze!" Lazlo shouted at the sprinting teenager. "Don't take another steppp, or you'll be sorry, you little brattt!"

Emmett ignored Lazlo and kept running down the hallway. This was Emmett's first really big mistake. You see, Lazlo Bleak was not the type of person who took kindly to being ignored, especially by teenage boys. So, basically being of an evil, twisted disposition, Lazlo did what is normal for someone of his crooked bent. Instead of trying to engage in dialogue and reason with Emmett[136], he chose a much more cowardly, violent alternative.

Lazlo unfastened the brass snap on his custom-made black leather holster, grabbed the gleaming, stainless steel, all-purpose[137], 12-inch blade resting along his thigh, and whipped it out. Like a circus knife-thrower[138], in one fluid motion, Lazlo sent the sharp dagger

---

136. *A nicer person would have held his left hand out flat and stuck his right hand perpendicular to it, thus forming the international time-out signal.*

137. *An all-purpose knife usually applied to cutting different types of foodstuffs, but it can also be applied to cutting different types of people.*

138. *In fact, for a few months, Lazlo worked for a Circus in Mexico where he was, in fact, employed as a knife thrower, but after killing several of his assistants, he gave up knife-throwing and decided to stick with being a geek who bites heads off chickens.*

straight toward the center of Emmett's back[139].

Emmett was still running after Hamlet, unaware that a deadly pointy projectile was flying at him. The knife twirled end-over-end through the air and with a sickening *thud*, the barbed point struck Emmett directly in the back of his neck.

But instead of piercing his flesh, the knife merely pressed slightly into his skin, and then, like a small child on a mini-trampoline, it popped back off, not leaving so much as a small scratch. The metal dagger clattered noisily to the floor. Emmett had hardly felt a thing.

However, Emmett did hear the din of the knife on the floor. He paused just long enough to look over his shoulder and, spotting the knife on the ground, to reach down and grab the blade, before taking off again

---

139. *It is* de riguer *for bad guys to knife you in the back, not face first.*

after his primate friend.

Everyone[140] was stunned. Their jaws dropped in unison. The blade had seemed to bounce off the kid as if he was made of Teflon. They all looked at each other, speechless.

Then Lazlo screamed, "Don't just stand there like idiotsss! Go after himmm! And get me backkk my knifffe!"

So, everybody took off after Emmett. Of course, they were all wondering why the bull-whip and the knife seemed to have no effect on him, but there was no time to stop and discuss this anomaly[141]. While Emmett raced to rescue Hamlet, Lazlo's gang raced to pulver-ize Emmett.

When Emmett ran into his Dad's lab,

---

140. *Except for Melvin, who was still unconscious and laying motionless on the ground.*
141. *An anomaly is something or someone out of the ordinary, which basically could encompass all the characters in this book.*

Hamlet was already there, swinging from the conical sonar transducer. Bobo was bouncing all over the lab after him, crushing test tubes and expensive sonic equipment. The entire lab was in shambles, but Emmett was just thankful Hamlet was still alive and in one piece.

Emmett yelled out "Hamlet!" and made the sign for taco.

Hamlet saw the sign, and Emmett knew he understood, because he could hear Hamlet's little primate tummy rumbling. It was at that moment that Bobo lunged at a distracted Hamlet and almost grabbed him, but the chimp jumped out of his grasp at the last second.

Then, Hamlet swung forward and landed in Emmett's arms. As Hamlet put his arms around Emmett's neck, Emmett felt both happy to be holding his friend and awful about lying to him. You see, Emmett didn't have a taco to give Hamlet. Emmett reached into his pocket and realized that all he had to offer his friend was an old gummy bear covered in hair and lint. Emmett handed the linty, hairy gummy bear to Hamlet, who popped it into his mouth and chewed.

Hamlet signed to Emmett, "Gummy. Tummy. Yummy."

Emmett looked at his friend and signed, "Okay, now, hold on, Hammy."

Hamlet held on tightly to Emmett as he ran up the winding staircase in the center of the lab. The iron steps spiraled up ten stories, ending at the rooftop observatory. Emmett took two steps at a time, propelling himself and Hamlet toward the roof.

By now, Lazlo, Marooshka, Fleo, the Don, and Joan all had arrived in the lab and joined

Bobo. Quickly, they moved to the base of the stairs. Bobo started to bounce up first, and the rest of them followed.

The freakish mob and Joan were gaining on him. But Emmett pushed on, climbing the iron steps, leaping as far and fast as he could and barely staying ahead of them. The instant Emmett reached the top, he swung open the rooftop observatory door and ran outside. He leaned in and tried to wedge the door closed, but before he could secure it, Marooshka barreled into the door and knocked it back open, sending Emmett and Hamlet flying into the air.

Emmett scrambled to his feet. Hamlet pounced onto his back again, wrapping his arms around Emmett's neck and his feet around Emmett's waist. As Lazlo and the rest of his coterie burst out of the door and onto the rooftop, Emmett waved Lazlo's knife back and forth. Emmett tried to look intimidating, but instead, ended up looking more like a young boy awkwardly waving a knife that was too big and heavy for him.

The ghostly glow of the full moon illuminated everybody as they moved around the rooftop—everybody, that is, except for Joan, who, with her short legs, was the only one still sprinting up the stairs. She hustled after them, her pigtails banging against the side of her sore neck as she ran. She couldn't slow down. She had to try to save the poor Redneck and this strange young boy she had just met.

As she reached the final step, she jumped through the rooftop door and surveyed the bizarre scene before her. Melvin's folding beach chair and his small plastic table were the only things standing between the knife-wielding boy with the chimp on his back and the angry horde trying to massacre them. Emmett and Hamlet were shrieking now, since they were both afraid of heights and had never been up to the top of the tower before. Joan jumped forward, stepping onto the white plastic table between Lazlo and Emmett.

She yelled, "Wait, please, friends. I'm confident there must be a viable[142] solution to this mayhem. Surely, we can talk this through and do an inspection in a more peaceful manner."

Emmett couldn't believe how naïve she was. He kept waving the knife at Lazlo and his gang, yelling at Joan, "Wake up! They're not inspectors. They want to eat Hamlet and kill me."

Joan responded, "Oh, I find that hard to

---

142. *A really good solution that is also do-able.*

swallow."

"It's the truth! They're here to eat him and kill us! Why else do you think they chased us up here—to see the moon?"

"Well, now that the rain has subsided, it 'tis quite a lovely night."

"Dude, c'mon, get outta the way, or you're gonna get hurt! PLEASE!"

Joan jumped off the table and moved to the rooftop's edge, next to Emmett.

Meanwhile, Lazlo's cronies yearned to move forward, but Emmett held them back with the large blade. Emmett could hear them breathing heavily. He could even hear the *splot, splot, splot* of the saliva dripping out of Lazlo's mouth and hitting the tarmac beneath them.

Marooshka said, "I vant to kill him. Can I kill him, boss? I really vant to. Please, boss, lemme—"

"No!" Lazlo protested. "Relax. There'sss no rush, Marooshka. He's nottt goinggg anywhere."

The Don snapped his tail at Emmett, but Lazlo caught it in his hands and signaled for all of his cohorts to step back.

"Nobody move. He'sss mine!"

"*Si, Senor Muy Macho,*[143]" The Don nodded. Then he shrugged, sat down against the tarmac, and pulled out an old, half-eaten chicken taco from his vest pocket.

Lazlo saw him and grew angry. He stepped forward, grabbed the taco[144] out of the Don's

---

143. *Mr. Really Macho or, at least, Mr. Thinks He Is Really Macho.*
144. *Please note the fact that The Don, a person of Latino descent, is eating a taco should not, by any means, imply that Latinos are lazy, ill-mannered, or only eat tacos. The truth is simply that The Don was evil and constantly ate tacos, unlike most Latinos, who are good, honest, hard-working people who eat all ethnicities of foods, including hot dogs and pizzas.*

hands, slammed it down on the folding plastic table, and said, "Don't eat nowwww!"

Lazlo looked over at Joan and said, "And you, my darlinggg, don't listen to thattt silly little boyyy. Thattt whole bittt aboutttt eating the chimppp was just a ploy... You see, it is against the by-laws of the Americannn Association of Language Labbbs to keeppp a chimppp, and we're merely here to rescue the poor creature."

"No way! He's full of it!" Emmett screamed.

Then, he stepped back against the railing, still slashing the knife frantically back and forth in front of him. He had to hold them off a little longer—long enough to hatch a plan. A masterful plan that could save them all[145].

Emmett thought and thought and thought.

---

145. *The problem was, and always is, it's so hard to think of a good plan when one is under such God-awful, life-threatening pressure.*

All the while, he kept scurrying along the rooftop railing, waving the big glistening knife in a menacing way. He was so focused on keeping Lazlo and his pack at bay, he almost stumbled over a thick black cable laying flat on the roof.

Yet, it was in that very moment, the moment in which he almost tripped and impaled himself on Lazlo's knife, that Emmett thought up the single greatest idea of his life.

Direct TV! His father had purchased an 18-inch Direct TV satellite mini-dish that was sitting facing east on the roof. The cable from the system swung from the base of the mini-dish all the way down to the ground outside the lab. His father had never paid the activation fee, so Emmett had never been able to watch all 678 stations and/or the pay-per-view options, but nevertheless, the cable itself was intact and led all the way down the side of the tower to the ground below. Hmmm... If only he could...

Emmett's plan was brilliant in its simplicity. Emmett would use sign language to communicate with Hamlet, instructing him to swing down the cable to safety. Then, Emmett could follow him. Once they got back down to the ground, they could hide in the Sulphur Swamp area and work together to defeat these evil mutants. It was ingenious. Inspired! Magnificent!

Emmett subtly started moving his hands, signing to Hamlet, "Jump to the cable!" Hamlet perceived that Emmett was signaling to him, nodded his head in understanding, and jumped.

However, instead of jumping to safety on

the thick black cable, as Emmett had intended, Hamlet jumped in the opposite direction onto the table where Lazlo had put The Don's taco. You see, even though Hamlet was one of the smartest Rednecks in the world, he was still learning sign language and tended to make mistakes, especially when he was hungry. In this instance, Hamlet misinterpreted the sign for "cable" as the sign for "table.[146]"

So, instead of swinging to safety on the cable, Hamlet jumped onto the table and grabbed The Don's taco. As he took his first big bite, Lazlo snatched him by the scruffy red hair of his neck.

Lazlo purred and smiled broadly, "Gottt you now, my little Redneckkk appetizerrr!"

As if that wasn't bad enough, Joan, who

---

146. *This might have been just wishful thinking on Hamlet's part, because on the table was a yummy little taco.*

also knew sign language and was standing close to Hamlet, thought Emmett was signing to her and not to Hamlet.

So, thinking Emmett was instructing her to "jump to the cable," she had done just that—she jumped!

Indeed, Joan threw herself over the railing and toward the cable running down the side of the tower. She sailed high into the air, reached for the cable, and grabbed it. Yes, she snagged hold of the cable and was safe...

That is, until a second later, when the cable snapped right off the mini-satellite dish bolted to the roof[147]. The appalling POP of the cable dislodging itself from the satellite dish so terrified Joan that she screamed and let go of the now loose cable. Within a nanosecond,

---

147. *Satellite TV cables are meant to support digital TV signals, not teenagers who seek thrills by swinging upon them.*

Joan, her legs flailing wildly, was falling silently toward the swamp thousands of feet below.

Emmett stared at her in disbelief. Why would anyone in their right mind jump off a rooftop? Now, this girl was falling to her death because she'd thought he had told her to jump. To make matters worse, Hamlet, his best friend, was being held captive by the most evil man in the world. How messed up could things get? What was Emmett to do?

It was clear that Joan was going to die if he didn't do something fast. He had no time to waste. Nobody, woman or man, mutant or human, could survive a 100 story drop into a swamp, and even if they did, the Humungos would surely eat what was left of their still-breathing, bloody remains.

Emmett screamed, "Noooo!" and threw himself through the air toward her falling body. What he would do with her once he caught up to her, he hadn't figured out yet, but he felt responsible and wasn't going to let her fall alone.

As she fell, Joan looked up to see that Emmett was flying toward her. He stretched and twisted his body as he valiantly attempted to grab her. Joan tried to control her limbs and grasp onto him, too, but the wind buffeted them both around so much that neither of them seemed able to clutch onto the other.

In one final burst of energy, Emmett stretched out his hands, but Joan was still too far away. If only she was a bit taller or her webbed fingers were just a bit longer. If only. If only.

For a second—a long, frozen second—they both watched in horror as their hands reached to within an inch of each other, and then, with one mighty gust of wind, they were blown apart.

To their inevitable deaths, they fell....

And fell...

And fell...

And fell...

CHAPTER TEN

Falling for Joan

From a purely objective point of view, things looked rather grim for Joan and Emmett. Essentially, they were both a second away from being instantly reduced to bloody piles of bone, skin, and teeth. Yes, of course, it would happen so fast they wouldn't feel much, but still, they would be dead, which, for most people, is a bad thing to be.

And as if being dead wasn't bad enough, after their deaths, they would not have a nice burial, but instead, they would serve as a midnight snack for the blood-thirsty

Humungos waiting with baited breath[148] in the swamp below.

But, this evening, Joan and Emmett did not die. They did not die, because a strange and wonderful thing happened.

Right before he and Joan crashed into the swamp, Emmett was so overcome with fear that he screamed more violently than he had ever done before, and his voice reached the highest octave that he had ever hit. It was in this sound range—a range higher than any human or even any dog could hear, a range even higher than when he reduced Lazlo and his cronies to their knees—that the miracle of Sulphur Swamp occurred.

And what a miracle it was! The incredibly high pitch of his voice literally created an air

---

148. *Baited breath might sound like it implies breath stinking of silverfish and night crawlers, but actually it implies deep-seated anticipation.*

cushion and reversed his fall. This allowed Emmett to defy gravity and FLY!

Yes, Emmett achieved acoustical levitation. A second before his body was about to be pulverized, his voice, the voice he had hated so much his whole life, saved his skinny little butt and Joan's butt as well. Like a bird or a plane or even Superman, Emmett held his arms out to his sides and used his voice to send himself soaring toward Joan. Just before she plummeted into the rocks, he swooped down, grabbed her in his arms, and jettisoned her back up into the sky.

Joan screamed with relief, "Merci boucoup[149] and wahoo-wahhh!"

A huge smile swept across her face as she hugged Emmett forcefully. She even planted

---

149. *French for* thank you very much. *The P at the end is silent, and if you say it out loud, the French police will chop off your tongue and French-fry it.*

a big, fat, sloppy, wet kiss on his cheek.
Though pecking Emmett's cheek was a sweet
and kind thing, it was not a smart thing to
do, for two very good reasons: One, Emmett
had not yet mastered acoustical levitation.
And two, Emmett had never been kissed by a
girl before.

In fact, Emmett was so taken
aback by the kiss that
he stopped scream-
ing, and they
both start-
ed falling
all   over
again. Yes, for
the second time with-
in five   seconds,
Emmett and Joan
were knocking on

the door to death's inner sanctum[150].
Fortunately, Emmett quickly cleared his
head and started screaming again.

Once more, he reversed their fall and pro-
pelled himself back up in the air. By using his
voice to levitate, Emmett was able to pull them
both to safety a millisecond before they would
have become a grisly heap of human wreckage.

As Emmett continued to scream and float
up through the air, he manipulated his vocal
cords, playing with the sound of his voice to
measure how it affected his flight path. As he
did, he noticed how hitting different notes
allowed him to move up and down. Quickly,
Emmett gained control over the sounds
escaping out of his mouth so that he could
control exactly how he moved through the

---

150. *A small ugly place that looks very much like a
dressing room at the Gap, but much, much
hotter and featuring posters of the Blues Clues
dog everywhere.*

sky. And the more he flew, the more he loved the pure ecstasy of free-style flight.

Joan loved it, too. She screamed with pleasure, "Higher! Faster! Ahhhh-ffirmative!"

It was bliss. Joan held on to Emmett tightly as he pierced the night sky, flying all the way back up to the top of the tower. They were going to live. They would save Hamlet and maybe even the whole world, although it could be months before Dr. Golem would be able to get his Direct TV cable hook-up repaired.

Emmett modulated his voice to lift them over the railing. Then, he hit a low, flat note that allowed them to hover only a few inches above the rooftop. Gradually, he softened his voice until they stopped floating and gently landed on the rooftop.

They both looked around and realized that the whole rooftop was deserted. Lazlo and his coterie of bad guys had chimp-napped Hamlet and taken off.

Emmett sprinted toward the stairs, "C'mon, let's see where they went."

Joan followed right behind him.

When they finally got down to the front entrance of the lab, Emmett pointed out at the driveway. Through the sliding glass front door, he and Joan could see the faint outline of the pickup and the Airstream speeding down the hill.

Emmett's first instinct was to use his voice to fly after them, but before he could open his mouth, he heard his father's moans of pain and knew he needed to stay and tend to him. Joan was already holding Dr. Golem's head in her lap as Emmett ran back over to them.

Emmett's father looked up at his son and said, "Sorry, Emmett. I should've recognized them. I let you and Hamlet down. Forgive me."

"It's okay, Dad. We'll get Hamlet back.... So, um, Dude, are you hurt?"

"I'm okay. Just a little bump on the old noggin. How about you? Did they hurt you?"

"Nope. Um, eh... Guess what? You know, like, what everybody says about acoustical levitation being a myth. Well, they're wrong."

A huge smile broke out over Dr. Golem's face. "I knew it! You flew, didn't you?"

"Yep, it was freaking great! You should've seen me."

"I wish I could've."

"Well, you will, Dad, you will. Now, um, like, I really need to go after Hamlet."

"Yes, but wait, kiddo. Before you go. There is one important thing I think we must do."

"What?"

"Help me up, and I'll show you."

Emmett bent down and took his father's hand.

CHAPTER ELEVEN

THE AWFUL TRUTH ABOUT EMMETT

Most children think of themselves as the center of the universe. But they are wrong. They are not the center of anything except their own little childish fantasies.

Toddlers, tweeners, teenagers, adults, seniors—we are all just tiny specks in a huge universe that will keep on going with or without us. This realization comes to most people in their twenties or thirties, and it is an essential part of being a grown-up. Of course, there are some horribly self-centered, immature people who never come to this realization at all[151].

Joan Paul came to this realization at the tender age of thirteen. For the first twelve years of her life, Joan had thought that growing up was a natural outgrowth of getting older. In other words, as one got older, they automatically grew up. Yet, ever since she came above deck, she was starting to see that this was not true at all[152]. Growing up had nothing to do with age. Many so-called "grown-ups" were merely overgrown children who wore large shoes, ate dessert before dinner without getting in trouble and could vote, but didn't.

After the events of the past two days, Joan was starting to see that life above deck was

---

151. *Just look at most politicians, movie stars, and sports figures.*
152. *Joan might have read a lot of Russian novels dealing with great themes, like love, death, and pumpernickel bread, but she really had little experience with the realities of growing up.*

much more complex than she had at first thought. A great deal of what she had been taught by her father didn't seem to hold water[153] anymore. For example, he had always told her that she should respect her elders, but many of the elders she had recently met did not merit respect. In fact, many were quite despicable human beings.

Joan realized that being a mature adult had nothing to do with age or experience or knowledge. A person could be forty or fifty or sixty and still not be a true "grown-up." Adults should not be judged by their age or by their IQs, but by the way they act and the way they treat strangers, animals, and defenseless, web-footed children.

Her whole life, Joan had believed that she,

---

153. *"To hold water" was one of Mr. Paul's favorite expressions to say, especially when he was passing water.*

more than anyone else in the world, had experienced true, deep pain. Over the past few days though, she had come to recognize that everyone above deck suffered. She was not alone in that department.

Despite what she may have fantasized or read about in books, growing up was neither fun nor easy. It was a painful process of sloughing off childish dreams. Like a snake shedding its skin, Joan saw that she would have to survive a series of tortuous moltings, until all that remained of her was a shiny, naked young adult, weary, but wiser.

Growing up was about suffering and then summoning the strength to move beyond that suffering. It was about facing her fears instead of running from them. It was about going above deck and staying there no matter how scary things might be. Losing her father, someone she loved, her only family, was excruciatingly hard, but this misfortune had also given her a renewed sense of her own inner strength.

No matter how dark things seemed, she realized that her father was still and always would be with her, in her heart. She seemed to hear his voice inside her head, reassuring her that she was going to be alright. His voice insisted she could make it, that even though all she'd been through above deck was not good or fun or easy, it was necessary for her to endure if she was to become a real grown-up.

And, she did have two new friends. Dr. Golem and Emmett were with her now, standing by her on the rooftop as they conducted a memorial service to help her lay her father's soul to rest.

The moon frowned down upon all three of

them as they held burning candles in their hands. No one spoke as the smoke from the candles' flames danced up to the heavens. In silence, they stood for a few more seconds.

Then Dr. Golem took a step forward and softly intoned, "We are gathered here tonight to pay tribute to Joan's father, Mr. Paul." Dr. Golem turned to Joan, "Sweetie, did he have a first or middle name I can use?"

She shook her head, "Not that I know of."

"You sure?"

"Affirmative."

"Um... Well, uh, Mr. Paul[154] was a good man and a good fisherman. He invented the much-loved bread-crumb-coated fish stick as well as the tasty condiment, tartar sauce. But most important, he was a good father who loved his daughter, Joan, very much. We are very sorry about what happened to him, and to be honest,

I feel horrible about it, since I was the one who initially bred those horrible Humungos—"

Joan stepped forward and rubbed Dr. Golem's arm. "Actually, Dr. G., please don't foist blame upon yourself. I take full responsibility. It was negligent of me to allow him to rush headlong into the swamp without first doing the proper research[155]. Speaking of which, do you think it is negligent of us to not alert the authorities?"

Dr. Golem responded, "No, Joan. At this point, I feel there is little they could do except create more problems for you, such as trying to put you in some type of institution or foster home. So, if you don't mind, I'd prefer to keep

---

154. *In truth, Mr. Paul's full name was Paul P. Paul, but for obvious reasons, he never told this to Joan or anybody else.*
155. *Joan's message here is clear: Do your homework or you, too, could experience the horribly painful sensation of getting lemon juice sprayed in your eyes and then having your skull chewed off by a huge female shrimp.*

this whole unfortunate incident to ourselves."

"Affirmative," Joan said.

Emmett looked at her. "I'm sorry, too. I was the one who dumped the Humungos into the swamp, so like, I also feel like it was my fault."

"Negatory, Emmett. It's not your fault, either."

"Well, if there is anything I can do to help, just tell me, okay?"

"Sure. Thanks." Joan smiled courageously.

"Joanie, is there anything you want to say about your father?" Dr. Golem asked.

Joan nodded and looked up at the heavens. "Father... Many times, you told me about how I was a foundling, and you took me in. You gave me a home. You called me daughter, and you loved me as if I were your own child. For that, I will be eternally grateful[156].

"Yes, I learned a great deal from my books, but I learned even more from you. You taught me that if God puts tartar on your teeth, don't fret, just make sauce out of it. You showed me that if you never cast your net out to the sea, you'll never catch anything. In other words, I learned from you my most important lesson: You can't hide away your whole life. It's hard and scary out here, but there comes a day when we all have to go above deck and stay above deck!

"And so, tonight, even though you have departed this world, you and all that you've taught me remain with me. I can still hear your voice saying, 'It's okay, my little veggie-wedgie. I will always love you and be with you.'"

Joan started to cry. Dr. Golem gave her his

---

156. *This is a fine example of why Joan is a role model for the youth of today. She took responsibility for her actions and always thanked people.*

hanky, "Here, sweetie."

"Thanks." Joan took the hanky and she wiped her tears away. "I know you will watch over me for the rest of my life. You treated me as an equal and respected me, even if my hands and feet might have been more webbed than yours. I love you, Poppa, and always will."

Joan started crying again. Dr. Golem took her in his arms and hugged her. Emmett, who hadn't even noticed Joan's webbed fingers before, now couldn't help staring at them as they clutched his father. As soon as he realized what he was doing, he looked away.

The memorial service went on for a few more minutes, and then Dr. G., Joan, and Emmett extinguished their candles and went inside, down the stairs, into the lab complex.

Joan, being a compulsive neat-freak, wanted to start cleaning up immediately, but Emmett wouldn't let her. He was anxious to rescue Hamlet and would have left right then and there. But his father forced him to go into the kitchen so they could at least have a little family meeting and something to eat before they took off.

Everybody sat around the kitchen table. Dr. Golem was still wearing his bathrobe. He slouched against the table, pressing a bag of frozen peas against a huge lump emanating from his skull. Even with the makeshift cold compress freezing the skin on his forehead, Dr. Golem was sweating profusely.

Joan sat on the seat next to the good doctor, munching on some baby carrot sticks. Emmett paced nervously around the kitchen until he could stand it no longer.

"C'mon, dude, can we hurry up? I mean,

like, Hamlet could be dinner by now. The longer we wait, the farther away he may be getting—"

Dr. Golem countered, "Emmett, please. Relax. Trust your dear old scientific genius father. Hamlet is okay, and finding him won't be a problem."

"How do you know that?"

Dr. Golem pulled a GameBoy out of his bathrobe pocket. "Look—"

Emmett screamed, "Dad, this is totally the wrong time for video games—"

"Emmett, please, trust me and take this." He handed the GameBoy to his son and said, "My boy, you are now holding the one and only prototype of a state-of-the-art, microchip-driven, ultrasonic tracking device[157]. It's the wave of the future. And, of course, I invented it."

Emmett stared at the device. A bright red

dot pulsed on the GameBoy's screen. "Huh? What are you talking about? That's just my old GameBoy."

"Negatory, Emmett."

Joan put down her carrot stick and said, "Correct me if I'm wrong, Dr. Golem, sir, but I think it's fair to assume that the gadget you just gave Emmett is, in fact, not really Emmett's old GameBoy, but, in fact, merely the GameBoy's exterior casing. It appears to me that you have, in actuality, removed the circuitry and replaced it with an ultramodern tracking sensor.

"In addition, since you are the caretaker of one of the last seventeen Rednecks in the world, I would also assume you have already

---

157. *Like Lo-Jack, Northstar, or any other GPS (global positioning satellite) system in a car, but in this case, it was in a chimp.*

implanted in your young primate's shoulder a state-of-the-art, ultrasonic microchip. This device most likely operates by bouncing sound waves off a satellite to the tracking device, thus allowing us to track Hamlet wherever he might be."

"Correctamundo!" Dr. Golem shouted. "You're a very sharp girl, Joan."

"Thank you, sir."

"However, you were wrong about one thing. I did not implant the chip in Hamlet's shoulder; I implanted it in his upper thigh."

Emmett said, "So, if it's still beeping, that means Hamlet's still alive and not that far away, right?"

"Exactamundo[158], my boy."

Emmett looked down at the beeping red dot and smiled. He collapsed into a chair, "Thank God! That's a relief! I couldn't understand how you could be so calm... So, okay, are we done with this family meeting, then?"

Dr. Golem tossed the frozen peas down on the table, got up out of his seat and nervously shuffled away from his son. "Well, there is one more thing, but we can do it some other time. Forget about it. Go find Hamlet. Here are my car keys.[159]" Dr. Golem pulled a set of keys out of his pocket and handed them to Emmett. "Have fun and don't stay out too late, kiddo."

Emmett slipped the GameBoy tracking device into his pocket and grabbed the keys. As he was about to run out of the lab, he paused for a second. Something did not feel right. Emmett stared at his father, "Dad, before I go, is there anything else I need to know?"

---

158. *A Spanish word that means correctamundo, but not exactly.*

Dr. Golem answered, "No. Nothing at all. Have a safe trip and go get that mischievous little Redneck. Have a safe trip. Bye-Bye."

Dr. Golem tried to exit quickly past his son, but Emmett slammed his right hand into the wall right next to his father's head. Dr. Golem then uneasily squirmed to the other side and Emmett smashed his left hand into that side of the wall, effectively pinning his father in place, like a mounted monarch butterfly in a science exhibit[160].

Emmett was not happy, not happy at all. He growled at his father, "Duuuuuude, before I go, I was hoping you could explain to me how I got whipped and knifed tonight, yet I don't even have a single scratch on my body?"

"Heh, heh, heh... Um, eh... Well, the men

---

159. *Since adults don't regularly hand out car keys to 16-year-old boys, it is clear that something was deeply disturbing Dr. Golem.*

in our family have very strong skin." Dr. Golem ducked his head and tried to pull away from his son.

Emmett did not let him move. "One other little thing, dude. Why don't I have any memories of my life before two years ago?"

"Um, well, c'mon Em, you know the story. We've gone over this a millions times. You had a bad accident and hit your head, and you lost all your long-term memory."

Emmett punched a hole in the kitchen wall. "That's garbage! Tell me the truth! There must be a reason. I know you know what it is. Why can I fly? Why can't I go to school? What happened for the first fourteen years of my life?"

"Emmett, please. Forget it. You don't want

---

160. *Notice the irony here, of the scientist becoming the science exhibit.*

to know."

"Yes, I do. Please tell me. It has to do with my mother, doesn't it?"

"Um. No... Not really..."

"Tell me!" Emmett completely lost control. He grabbed his father and held him up in the air. A high-pitched trilling sound came out of his throat. His fingers closed around his father's neck, and they both rose a few feet into the air.

Dr. Golem groaned in pain, "Aaaaaaarggghhhh!"

After just losing her own father, Joan couldn't stand to watch Emmett commit patricide[161]. So, she ran over and pulled on Emmett's legs. "Please, gentlemen, there's been enough violence here for one night!"

---

161. *Killing your own father or someone named Pat. Obviously, in this case, Dr. Golem was not named Pat, so it would be the former and not the latter.*

Emmett glanced over at her and realized she was right. He let go of his father, who fell to the floor, a broken shell of a scientist. Emmett closed his mouth and landed back on the ground. He looked down at his father and felt horrible. How could he have almost killed him his own father? What was he thinking? What had gotten into him? Emmett fell to his knees and started sobbing.

Dr. Golem whispered to Joan, "Thank you." Then, he

looked down at his son and said, "Emmett, kiddo, I'm sorry. I don't know what to say."

"Just say the truth."

"Okay... I'm— I'm not really your father."

Emmett wiped his eyes and said, "What are you talking about? Of course you're my father."

"Well, actually, I'm really more like your step-dad... I— I— I bought you."

Emmett rose to his feet, "You bought me?!"

"Yes, and you weren't cheap. I spent my entire life savings to have my old college roommate at Cal Tech make you. He's this surfer/scientific genius whose great with cybertronics. And I told him not to finish your voice box, so I could tweak it to achieve acoustical levitation. But after spending months futzing with your vocal cords, all I thought I'd accomplished was to mess up your voice. That's one of the reasons why I've been so depressed these past couple of years. Although now, if what you said is true, I guess I didn't fail after all... Pretty cool, huh?"

"No! It's not cool!" Emmett yelled. "You told me I had a mother and that she died giving birth to me."

"I'm sorry. The manual told me to tell you that."

"What manual?"

"The one you came with. See, as an android, you were basically a clean slate when I got you, and well, I kinda got lazy and didn't get around to programming your memory. It's a lot of work. So, I decided the best thing to do was to tell you that your mother died during childbirth, and that, well, you had a horrible accident at school when you were fourteen and lost all your memory—"

"So, I have no mother, and I was really born two years ago?"

"Yep."

"This is unbelievable. NO WAY! STOP! So, like, even if this were the truth, how does it explain the fact that knives and whips and nails can't go into my skin?"

"Well, you were created with a titanium-based sub-epidermis[162] that feels natural, but is practically impermeable. That's why the whip and knife and nails didn't penetrate your skin. To be honest, I was never really sure how strong your skin was, but I never had the heart to test it. Although, clearly, my buddy at Cal Tech did a great job with you."

"I thought you said you were going to tell me the truth? I don't believe any of this."

"It's the truth, Em. Look, you know how depressed and lonely I get up here in the lab.

---

162. *Sub-epidermis is the layer beneath the skin, in science-talk.*

So, I thought maybe having a child would help. I mean, I tried dating, but no woman would ever stay with me.

"Then, I thought to myself, if I could create a sonic transducer, why couldn't I create my own child, too? And I tried, but, well, I failed. So I called up my old college buddy, and he whipped you up for me in a few weeks. I vowed you would be my greatest living language experiment. But after awhile, I felt really bad about working on you, and I got scared that I might do something to harm you. I couldn't risk it; the last thing in the world I wanted to do was hurt you. That's also the reason I never let you go to school. You have to believe me. I was just grateful to have you as my son and my friend."

Dr. Golem started weeping, and then Emmett started to cry, too.

Emmett wiped away his tears, turned away from his father, and screamed, "No, you're lying. You're such a liar! I am human. I know I am."

"No," Dr. Golem shook his head. "It all makes sense now, doesn't it? The lack of memories. The toughness of your skin. How you hurt those people in Africa with your voice. How you flew—"

Emmett walked away from his father and jangled the car keys in his hand. "Whatever! I'm going to rescue my best friend. And once I get Hamlet, you know what, I'm never coming back!"

Emmett stormed out of the kitchen. Dr. Golem watched him go and crumbled onto the linoleum like an old burlap sack of rotten potatoes.

Joan grabbed the rest of her carrot sticks

and ran after Emmett. "Wait, Emmett. Please. I want to go with you."

She ran after him as fast as she could. In the foyer, she caught up to him. Joan grabbed him by the sleeve and yanked. He twisted around and glared at her. "No. Leave me alone. You should go back home."

"I don't have a home anymore. I want to go with you. I need to go with you. Please, I beg of you."

"What's it to you? Hamlet's not your friend."

"No, not yet... but you are."

"We just met."

"You saved my life."

"You're too young. You could get hurt."

"Not if I'm with you. I feel safe with you. You're kind and sensitive and good-hearted. You noticed my webbed fingers, and you didn't comment upon them. *Sil vous plais*[163]— allow me to go with you. I can be of great assistance. Think about it. We're both freaks. Outsiders. Mutants. We should be together."

Emmett pulled away from her, "No, it'll be too dangerous. You can live here from now on, with my dad."

"Your dad is a gentleman, but negatory, Emmett. Look, I might be capable of covering my vast insecurities with an even vaster vocabulary, but underneath all my fancy rhetoric[164], I'm really just a frightened little girl who's scared to death, especially of being alone. Just like Hamlet is right now, and you aren't deserting him. Affirmative?"

---

163. *Again, she is resorting to using French. Clearly, Joan really, really wants Emmett to let her go with him.*
164. *Fancy language. For instance, look at the beautiful way these footnotes are written, and then you'll understand.*

"Yeah."

"You'd do anything for him. Affirmative?"

"Yeah, affirmative. But what does that have to do—"

"It has to do with friendship, Emmett. Friends don't leave friends behind—"

"Yeah, but—"

"No buts! My whole life has been spent hiding below deck. When I finally ventured above deck a few days ago, you were the only person I met who didn't try to take advantage of me. Your actions demonstrated your true friendship. I've never had a friend before. Ergo, thus, and hence, to demonstrate my reciprocal friendship with you, I feel it is incumbent upon me to go with you. So, please allow me?"

Emmett looked at her—a little, pigtailed girl with big cat-eye glasses, skinny legs, and webbed hands. The rhinestones on her glasses sparkled in the fluorescent light. Her green eyes begged him and tore at his heart. What the heck was he supposed to say or do? How could he resist?

Of course, he couldn't resist. Not this girl. Not on this day. Emmett had no choice but to succumb. And as he did, he got the sense that this was only the beginning of the problems he'd be facing with women for the rest of his life.

For dramatic effect, Emmett waited another moment and then he said, "Alright, dude. C'mon. But you should know... I, uh, er, um... I have chronic gastritis. Okay, there, I said it."

"Well, I have chronic anosmia.[165]"

"What's that?"

"I have no smelling capability. I also have weak hearing and poor eyesight."

---

165. *Smelling loss which should really be called* **anosemia**, *but it isn't.*

"Cool!" Emmett laughed. "Oh, yeah, and one other thing. Um, eh, you have to promise never to say a word about that whole android thing."

"I promise. Affirmative."

"Okay... Wait a second, dude. You also have to promise not to talk like such a dweeb. So, stop saying dorky words like 'negatory' and 'affirmative.'"

"Affirma—I mean, okay..."

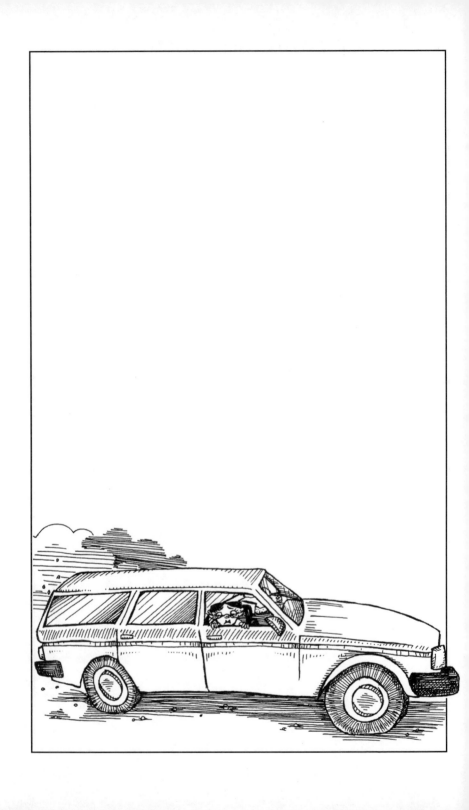

CHAPTER TWELVE

JOAN OF ARKANSAS

Beep-beep-beep! The red dot on the GameBoy ultrasonic tracking device started pulsing so fast and chirping so loudly that it woke Joan up from her nap. She wiped away the spittle that had collected on the side of her face and tried to fix her hair. Emmett didn't seem to notice. He was too busy alternating his gaze between the road and the tracking device while trying to keep his Dad's '86 blue Volvo from crashing into a tree.

After driving south for nine hours, Emmett was exhausted. However, when he suddenly inhaled the fresh briny scent of the intra-coastal waterway and the Gulf of Mexico, the adrenaline started pumping in his veins[166] and he felt reinvigorated. Meanwhile, the increasingly quick beats of the tracking device mimicked Joan's racing heartbeat. Hamlet was definitely still alive, and it seemed like they were finally getting close to rescuing him.

But they could not be reunited with Hamlet until they overcame five major problems—a certain evil villain by the name of Lazlo Bleak and his four mean-spirited colleagues.

The next few hours were going to be tense. Very tense. Maybe even fatal. But Emmett and Joan were resigned to do whatever it

---

166. *Since he is an android, he doesn't really have adrenaline or veins, but it is a nice turn of a phrase, and he does have a mercury-based psuedo-adrenaline that flows through his admantium bones. So there!*

took to save Hamlet. If that meant dying, they were resolved to do that, too, although they both preferred to stay alive, if possible.

The Louisiana sun shone down on the Volvo, reflecting into Emmett and Joan's eyes. Emmett wore cool wraparound sunglasses that were partially shrouded by the hair falling across his face. Joan squinted behind her retro cat-eye glasses. She wished she had some sort of clip-on tinted lens attachment for them, but alas, she did not.

Joan squeezed her eyes into narrow slits and searched the area for familiar landmarks. She seemed to recognize where they were. The smell. The foliage. The dirt road. It was Hackberry.

They had followed the pulsing dot all the way back to Hackberry and were now driving up to the dock where Joan's father's old trawler was still moored. Why in the world would Lazlo return here? Joan knew trouble was afoot, big trouble, but she could not, for the life of her, put her webbed finger on exactly what Lazlo was up to.

Joan yanked on Emmett's sleeve. "Emmett, look. Isn't that Lazlo's pickup and Airstream? *Sil vous plais*[167], pull over and park in the shade of that tree. Hurry."

Emmett hid the car under a huge Spanish oak. Joan pointed at Lazlo's trailer in front of her father's trawler. Emmett and Joan watched as Lazlo screamed at Marooshka and Bobo, as they carried a large steel-barred cage out of the back of the Airstream. Lazlo directed them toward the trawler, and they carried the cage up a gangplank and onto the boat. As Emmett

---

167. *Again, more French. Clearly, Joan is at her wit's end here.*

and Joan strained to see what was going on, they both noticed that there was something in the cage. Something moving. It was Hamlet. He was alive and frantically jumping around.

What should Emmett and Joan do? How could they help him? They had driven for nine hours, but neither of them really had thought about what they would do if, in fact, they actually did find Hamlet and Lazlo.

They needed a plan. And, hopefully, one that was much better than Emmett's previous "let's-grab-onto-an-old-cable-and-hope-we-don't-fall-to-our-death" strategy. But what could a skinny 13-year-old girl and her 16-year-old android friend possibly do to combat the pure evil of Lazlo Bleak and his sideshow cronies?

Emmett looked at Joan and whispered, "Hey, dude, you're the genius whose read a million books. How the heck are we supposed to rescue Hamlet?"

Joan looked serious. "Well, I shall need a moment to cogitate[168] over this predicament?"

"Huh?"

"I need time to think, merci bocoup.[169]"

"Okay, dude. Whatever. Let's open up our windows and try to hear what they're up to."

They rolled down their windows and sat in silence, staring at their caged primate friend a mere 100 yards away, yet still far from their warm embrace and safety.

Marooshka and Bobo maneuvered around the ship, finally dropping Hamlet's cage onto the bow of the deadly still trawler with a loud *clang*.

From their hiding spot in the Volvo, Joan

---

168. *To think, in Joan talk, and also, to rotate cogs in the mind's machinery.*
169. *Pronounced mare-see-bow-coo by you and you and you…*

and Emmett stared at Hamlet in his little metal-barred prison. He looked so miserable. He was a caged beast, an object to be ogled, a new side-show exhibit: Hamlet, the Ameslan talking chimp.

Suddenly, almost as if he could sense Emmett and Joan nearby, Hamlet grabbed hold of the steel bars and started howling, "Waaaaaaooooooooooh!"

Lazlo and his gang ignored the noise. The Don strolled over to Lazlo, "So, Senor Impresario, when do we eat? I have waited long for this comida exotica and am mucho hungry."

Lazlo spun around and glared at him, "You idiottt! We can't eat that Redneckkk now! He's trained to speakkk. He's worth much more as a side-show curiosityyyy than a mealll. We musttt exhibit himmm!"

"Si, but I thought we were going to have dinner? My tummy is growling!"

"Imbecile! Because of you and your stupid-dd, growlinggg, taco-eating tummy, Joan is deaddd! My webbed star is muerto! And so we can't eat that stupiddd Redneck, he'sss going to be our new side-show freakkkk!"

Queen Fleopatra ambled over to them and said, "Lazlo, Senor Frijoles, vhat seems to be the problem here?"

Lazlo answered, "This scaly moron failsss to understand that when my little Joan jumped off the roofff and killed herselfff, we lost the biggest attractionnn in the worlddd of teratology since Zippy the Pinheaddd![170] Millionsss! I could have made millionsss off that little webbed girl. People would have come from nearrr and farrrr to see the webbed-fingereddd and -footeddd girl I was goinggg to call, JOAN OF ARKANSAS![171]"

Back in the Volvo, Emmett looked over at Joan, "Cool name. I love it—Joan of Arkansas."

The sides of Joan's neck started aching again. She swung her head away from Emmett, her pigtails bopping him as she spoke, "But, I'm not from Arkansas. I grew up in Love Canal."

---

170. One of the all-time great side-show freaks, who was seen by millions of people over the course of his illustrious career. He wasn't a true pinhead, but acted like one for the sheer joy of it. He also had one of the top two worst haircuts in modern history.
171. Obviously, a play upon the name Joan of Arc, who was a bi-polar 16-year-old French girl who stopped taking her Prozac and started hearing voices, wearing men's clothing, and had the other of the top two worst haircuts in history.

"But Joan of Arkansas sounds good. Heroic-like."

"It's a misnomer[172]. I detest it."

"Whatever, dude, chill out, the main thing now is, we need a plan to rescue Hamlet and to get your dad's boat back. So, got any smart ideas?"

"Actually, as we speak, I do not, but give me a moment and I shall devise one of a plethora of plots that might be appropos.[173]"

"Huh?"

"Sorry. Please forgive me. I have very little experience with social interaction. But maybe this will be a good exercise for us in collaboration and devising strategems.[174]"

---

172. *Meaning, the wrong word. Like going into Burger King and asking for a Big Mac.*
173. *Again, Joan with the French. This word means appropriate, and the S at the end is silent and does not belong there, but is there for some unknown reason.*
174. *Strategems are like strategies, but they are semiprecious.*

"Say what?"

"Let us ask ourselves: What do we know about Lazlo?"

"Hey, you tell me. You're the one who drove with the guy for nine hours. What's he like?"

"He seemed especially fond of disco music."

"No way! Seriously?"

Joan nodded her head, "Affirma—I mean, yep."

"He's really sick, huh?"

"I am not a licensed practicing psychoanalyst, but it's safe to say that in most therapeutic circles, he would clearly be diagnosed as having serious maternal phobias."

"In English?"

"Mother issues. I cannot conclusively validate this hypothesis, but I would venture to assert that Lazlo's mother is a dead gypsy fortune-teller, who, to this day, haunts him, especially at night."

"Hmmm. Okay. Don't exactly know how that might help though, but thanks for sharing..."

"If you don't mind, I'd appreciate a few moments of unmolested silence for deeper thought."

Emmett nodded and closed his mouth.

Joan pulled on her pigtails[175] and thought. She always founded that yanking her pigtails activated dormant brain cells and helped her concoct great ideas. And to her utter delight, her pigtail-yanking-method worked. A brilliant sparkle emanated from her sea green eyes as a brilliant idea germinated in her head. "Eureka!" She yelled.

---

175. *If you are a boy without pigtails who is searching for a good idea, it might be tempting to yank your sister's pigtails or the hair of the pigtailed girls in school, but don't do it. It is mean-spirited and hurtful...*

She sat bolt upright in the passenger seat of the Volvo and grabbed Emmett's arm, making him jump up in the air.

"Ah-ha! Correct me if I'm wrong, my friend, but from our eavesdropping it seems evident that Lazlo believes that you and I are deceased. Affirma— I mean, right?"

"Yeah."

"That also means he doesn't know you can achieve acoustical levitation."

"FLY! I can fly, just say it—"

"Actually, I beg to differ. True flight and acoustical levitation are based upon two very different aeronautical conceits —[176]"

"Enough. Okay. Whatever. Just tell me your point?"

---

176. *Acoustical levitation uses sound waves for flight, while what we know of as true flight is based upon a manipulation of airwaves which may cause sound waves, but aren't sound waves.*

"I've got a plan. Back up the car. We need to go into town and buy some supplies. Then, we can come back tonight."

"But, dude, are you sure they'll still be here?"

Joan stuck her thumb out of the window and tested the wind. "Yes. Fortunately, the wind is practically nonexistent; hence, thus, and ergo, sailing away is not an option. In addition, activating the trawler's engine will be quite difficult, considering I hold the only spare key. Furthermore, I also hold the only spare key to the motorized anchor-retrieval winching system.[177]"

"Okay, cool. So, they aren't going any-where, huh?"

"I would venture to say that you are correct!"

"Alrighty, then! Let's rock and roll!"

---

177. *A powerful device that pulls the anchor out of the sea with a winch, which is like a powerful witch, but only more reliable and less dependent on secret potions.*

THE GHOST OF LAZLO'S MOTHER

The soft glow of the moon illuminated Lazlo and his coterie as they sat on molded plastic lawn chairs positioned around the steel cage on the deck of the trawler.

Lazlo was staring up at the moon, wishing that he had one of those "ultraviolent," purple, glowing bug zappers which he could hang from the ship's boom. There was nothing he liked better than spending a warm night watching moths and mosquitoes fry themselves on its ultra-hot purple surface. Zizzzzz! Lazlo loved the sound and smell of burning insects.

Yet, inevitably, whenever he bought one and brought it along on tour, just when a nice big pile of dead bugs had collected underneath the zapper, Fleo would get upset, utter a series of curses at him in Egyptian, and use Marooshka's bullwhip to lash out at the zapper until it was cracked and broken.

Lazlo lifted up his dinner and took a bite. It was a dreadful meal—a single slice of bologna with mayo on batter-whipped Wonder Bread. Fleo, Marooshka, The Don, and Bobo also sat nearby, eating bologna[178] sandwiches. No one spoke; they just chewed and slurped cans of diet soft drinks[179]. Clearly,

---

178. *The main ingredient in bologna is so truly grotesque that it shall remain nameless. However, there are many who claim that it is really the chopped remains of children who don't brush their teeth before they go to sleep at night.*
179. *As performers, they were all constantly watching their weight.*

nobody was pleased with this pathetic meal.

Lazlo peered inside the steel cage, illuminated only by the glow of the moon. Hamlet was inside, balled up in the fetal position, apparently sleeping.

Still munching on his sandwich, Lazlo spoke, "So, Don—"

"The Don, por favor."

"You claimmm to be a mechanical geniusss, yet, it appearsss as if you can't get the engine starteddd?"

"Without a key, it is muy difficult. Tomorrow, I will try to hotwire it. Si?"

Lazlo was not appeased. "And you, Bobo, what seemsss to be your problemmm activating the anchorrr-retrievalll winching systemmm?"

Bobo spoke quickly, as though he had just downed a truckload of frappuccinos. "Sorry, boss. Sorry. Need key. No work without key.

Can't lift. Back hurt. Sorry, boss. Sorry. Need key. Heh, heh, heh... Too heavy to lift by hand!"

Lazlo glared at Marooshka. "Too heavy, and yettt, we happen to have the world's strongesttt beardeddd lady righttt here on boarddd this crummy little trawlerrr."

Marooshka smiled at Lazlo, "You vant. I lift."

She put down her sandwich and walked over to the thick iron chain that sprouted out of the top of the boat and dangled down into the water. Marooshka stood over the chain and went into her pre-weight-lifting ritual. She did a double-bicep flex; stroked her beard; smelled her perspiring, hairy armpits; slapped her palms together with a Fwapp!; and screamed, "Marooshka Oofffka!"

As she hollered, she bent her knees, keeping her back ramrod-straight[180], and gripping

---

180. *A fine example of how important it really is to keep your back straight when lifting heavy objects.*

the chain in her callused palms, she pulled...

And pulled...

And pulled...

The veins and muscles in her legs started to quake. Though the combination of the heavy anchor and the force necessary to drag it up through thirty feet of water was tremendous, Marooshka was up to the task. She had the horsepower. She could do it. She was stronger than any man-made anchor-retrieval winching system. Her muscles were rock-hard cables trained to perform superhuman feats of strength.

And so, with a mighty burst of energy, she yanked the anchor from its nesting place at the bottom of the sea. Hand over hand, she slowly pulled the anchor up from the briny depths. It was a feat of awesome power. With quick wheezy exhales, she strained and tugged. As she lifted more and more of the chain out of the water, she dropped the linked lengths next to her on the bow, forming a large circular pile of chain.

Finally, she extricated the final link of chain, and the anchor broke through the surface of the water. Marooshka grabbed the anchor and held it above her head in triumph, exalting in her magnificent display of fortitude.

"How about a hand for Maroooshka Ooofkaaa, eh?!" she bellowed and bowed.

But before anyone could clap, a keen, trilling sound joined her voice. It was a high-pitched, unearthly tone— scary, yet also vaguely familiar. The eerie tone seemed to come from a ghostly apparition that had suddenly appeared in the sky above the trawler.

Lazlo stepped back in horror. The ghost wore a long flowing skirt, a silver-coined belt and silver-coined chains, a baggy white blouse, and multi-colored scarves wrapped around its head.

It looked like a flying gypsy fortune-teller. It looked like... Lazlo's mother[181].

Lazlo screamed in utter horror, "No, Mommmma! Nooooo!"

Maroooshka was so stunned to see a flying gypsy that she just stood there, staring at the specter, her jaw agape. Her arms and legs vibrated as she held onto the anchor.

Hamlet awoke from his slumber, saw the phantasm, and started howling. Fleo's fleas buzzed frantically, and then, in unison, fled en masse[182] behind Fleo's back. Bobo was so frightened that he bounced below deck. The Don grabbed all the sandwiches and followed Bobo.

---

181. *Or at least what one would imagine his mother looking like.*
182. *As in the movement of one massive mass.*

Lazlo dropped to his knees. "No, Momma, please! I willl be a good boy! Don't hurttt meeee! Pleassse!"

The flying gypsy[183] spoke in a high-pitched voice that seemed to crack. "I will not hurt you if you set the Redneck free!"

Lazlo nodded, "Yesss, Momma, yesss. Anything you say! Just don't hurttt meee! PLEASE!"

"Do it!" the apparition barked. "Now!"

Lazlo nodded and sprinted over to the cage. He pulled out a set of keys and unlatched the lock. He swung the steel gate open and tried to liberate Hamlet, but the Redneck chimp was too scared to move and just kept howling as he held onto the bars of the cage.

---

183. *These days, the word gypsy is not generally used, because it has negative connotations, but Lazlo, who is an evil man, called his mother a gypsy, so that is what she must be called.*

While all of this was happening, Joan stealthily emerged from under the Spanish oak and tiptoed up the gangplank and onto the trawler. Thus, she was right behind the cage when Lazlo opened it up. In fact, she was in the perfect position to snatch Hamlet and run back to the car.

But she couldn't snatch Hamlet as long as he was still in the cage. And even though the cage door was open, Hamlet did not seem to want to leave, especially with a scary gypsy ghost flying above him.

Suddenly, the gypsy ghost started to move her hands in the air. If Lazlo's eyes weren't deceiving him, it appeared as though the gypsy ghost was talking to Hamlet in sign language.

Yes, Lazlo was convinced of it now. The gypsy ghost was using sign language to urge the Redneck out of the cage. The more he thought about it, the more sure he was that his mother didn't know sign language. And her voice, well, it was totally wrong. He also remembered her being a heck of a lot shorter.

That was when Lazlo figured out what was really going on. True, Lazlo was a lot of things. Evil. Smelly. Superstitious. Greedy. And yes, he might have had mother issues and been afraid of ghosts, especially gypsy ghosts that looked like his mother and wanted to kill him. But Lazlo was not stupid! And that is exactly why the gypsy phantom should never have used sign language skills. Sure, it's tempting when you're trying to communicate with an Ameslan-speaking Redneck, but still, resorting to sign language was the gypsy's fatal mistake.

Just because Lazlo had figured out exactly what was going on didn't mean he wanted anybody else aboard the ship to know that he knew. So, still pretending to be scared, Lazlo moved to the gypsy ghost and said, "Motherrr, pleassse, I can'ttt get the chimppp out of the cage. Come down here and helppp me take the Redneckkk out of the cage."

The gypsy nodded and landed on the deck. Then, she stepped into the cage and whispered something to Hamlet. Instantaneously, Hamlet jumped into the gypsy's arms, as if he had known the gypsy his whole life. Just before the gypsy and Hamlet could step out of the cage, Lazlo swung the door closed in a vicious, malicious effort to lock them both in.

Fortunately, the gypsy noticed Lazlo's villainy and stuck her leg in between the swinging gate and the iron cage bar. With a loud clang, the bar smashed into her leg and did not close. This kind of cruel blow might have crippled the average ghost or person, but it did not seem to affect this gypsy. It was as though her leg had a titanium-based sub-epidermis or something of that ilk.

The gypsy, with Hamlet wrapped around her chest, threw open the gate, stepped out of the cage, and walked toward the side of the boat. But before the gypsy could fly away, Lazlo rushed at her.

"Get him! Stop him! Kill him!" Lazlo screamed, "That's not my mother, that's Golem's stupiddd boy from the labbb in draggg[184]!"

Yes, the gypsy really was Emmett, wrapped up in scarves and using his acoustical levitation to float in the air above the trawler. The scheme he and Joan had concocted consisted of having Emmett in gypsy clothes scare Lazlo into releasing Hamlet. Then, Joan would snatch Hamlet, and they would all meet at the Volvo under the Spanish oak and escape. Unfortunately, as with many of the best-intentioned plans, things went a bit awry[185], and everything came crashing down to Earth in a colorful pile of silver coins, scarves, and Redneck howls.

Queen Fleo jumped forward, coming to Lazlo's aid. With a "Fleshkadicka, milkadicka!"

---

184. *This means to dress like a girl, and it is popular among many Americans, especially high-ranking FBI agents.*
185. *Awry sounds like a type of sandwich bread, but it is really when things go screwy.*

she sent her army of fleas after Emmett, who was busy reopening his mouth to re-achieve acoustical levitation. Of course, the fleas went straight into his open mouth. Sacrificing themselves for their beloved queen, many a talented flea died in Emmett's salivary juices and esophagus, but they did not die for naught[186].

Fleo's fleas succeeded in keeping Emmett from screaming and uttering the proper tones to fly away. Without being able to achieve acoustical levitation, Emmett had no choice but to run. Holding tightly onto Hamlet, he sprinted across the trawler to the Volvo.

---

186. *Like nothing, but even less than nothing.*

Unfortunately, Emmett didn't get very far, because the first step he took was into the center of Marooshka's large iron circle of chains. This would not have been disastrous had he had stepped into the circle of chains just a moment or two sooner. But as it was, just as he put down his foot, Marooshka tried to throw the anchor at him, causing her biceps to rip and roll up both her arms like closed window shades, and even bursting a blood vessel in her left temple[187]. Blood spurted out of her forehead, and she collapsed, dropping the anchor back into the sea, which yanked up the chain, instantaneously forming a cold, cruel iron manacle around Emmett's ankle.

As Emmett screamed, Hamlet clutched

187. *This occurs frequently with strength athletes who eat too many healthy foods and protein shakes. So, avoid protein-based smoothies!*

him tightly. But the iron chain's grip on Emmett's ankle was even tighter and dug into his sub-epidermis as it pulled both Emmett and Hamlett off the trawler.

Emmett and Hamlet flew into the air and splashed into the intracoastal waterway.

CHAPTER FOURTEEN

A WARM WATERY GRAVE

For many, a fall of ten feet into a warm body of water would be a refreshing thing, but for Emmett and Hamlet, it was horrifying. Horrifying for Hamlet, because he had a deep-seated fear of falling. And horrifying for Emmett, owing to the fact that, because he had never gone to school, he had never learned how to swim, and thus, he was sure he was destined to drown.

Of course, all Hamlet had to do was let go of Emmett and swim to the surface. But he was so scared, he couldn't think rationally and refused to let go.

And even if Emmett had been an Olympic-caliber swimmer, there was still no way in heck he could swim back up to the water's surface with a 300-pound anchor pulling him straight down to the ocean's floor.

So, Emmett lost his mind and panicked. He desperately tried to pull himself back to the surface. He screamed and hollered under-water, but only succeeded in swallowing a few gallons of dirty saltwater. And no matter how he struggled, all he succeeded in doing was sink, slowly, inexorably down...

Down...

Down...

Joan watched from the dock as Emmett and Hamlet descended to the ocean floor. Even though one was an ape and the other was an android, still, they both needed oxygen to survive, and it was mighty hard to get oxygen underwater. Though Emmett's vocal cords might have saved him from certain death just the day before, unfortunately, sound doesn't travel well underwater, so his voice couldn't save him this time. There was no way out of this one. Emmett and Hamlet would both suffocate within three minutes.

And so, even though she wasn't wearing a swimming suit or a life jacket, and even though in fact, she was scared of water, Joan took off her glasses, slipped them into her pocket and dove in after them. Emmett and Hamlet were drowning and she had to try to help them.

Unfortunately, Joan did not know how to swim. Like Emmett, she had not gone to school, and thus, she had never received swimming lessons[188]. And though Mr. Paul

---

188. *See how important it is to go to school in order to survive in this cold, cruel world.*

had, on several occasions, tried to urge her above deck to give her a little swim lesson, she had always refused.

As she dove underwater, she deeply regretted refusing to come above deck for swimming instruction. She also regretted not thinking of a better plan than just diving in headfirst. The previous evening, she had jumped off the rooftop headfirst and almost died in the process. Now, it looked like her second big dive would surely be her last.

Joan vowed to herself that if she survived this ordeal, she would most definitely read more books about emergency response skills. Unfortunately, it was a little too late to go to the Hackberry library. Water was filling her lungs. She couldn't swim, and she couldn't breath—a deadly combination. And much to her chagrin, she was sinking fast.

Meanwhile, Emmett's lungs felt as though they were about to burst. With his last ounce of energy, he tried to push Hamlet away from him and to the surface. He tried signing to him "Swim! Swim, Taco-Breath!" But Hamlet just held on to him even tighter.

So, they were both doomed. Hamlet had decided that if he was going to go, he wanted to die with Emmett. It was a brave sentiment and also rather silly, but Redneck's are nothing if not loyal to the end.

Emmett and Hamlet gave up and accepted the inevitable. Then, just as the harsh, suffocating fingers of death started to close around them, Emmett and Hamlet noticed a skinny young girl in boots and a black dress swimming down toward them.

Emmett smiled broadly and thought, Joan really is a good friend. And pretty cute, too.

He even thought that he might love her...

Either way, he was glad he had brought her along.

Like a lead anvil, Joan dropped to the ocean floor, where Hamlet and Emmett were hovering by the anchor. How long could any of them hold their breath before they passed out? Ten more seconds? Twenty more seconds?

The blood pounded in Joan's head. The sides of her neck throbbed and seemed to be opening up. Blood poured out of slits in her neck. If she didn't drown soon, she would surely bleed to death. Like her father, she was destined to die in the water. She had come from the sea, and she was fated to die in the sea.

Her lungs felt ready to explode. Her heart pounded to the point of rupturing. She needed air. Fresh air. Oxygen. The pressure was too much. Her lungs couldn't take it. Her heart was

screaming. Death would be a welcome friend.

No! She shook her head. She could not think of death right now. She had work to do. She needed to pull the chains off of Emmett's foot.

But she couldn't. They were wrapped too tightly. She struggled, but she was just not strong enough.

She thought of abandoning Emmett and Hamlet, of using her last bit of precious energy to swim back to the surface and at least save herself.

But, she couldn't do that to her two friends. She had to help them, but it was so hard to do anything without air. She had absolutely no ener-gy left in her

body. She had lost too much blood through the slits in her neck. All she felt was pain. Too much pain. She had no choice. She gave in and succumbed to the warm embrace of death.

It was fate—three young friends, all destined to drown together.

Then, suddenly, the blood pouring out of the sides of her neck started to coagulate and harden. Yes, it was as though the slits on the sides of her neck had somehow instantaneously healed, leaving in their place, not a scab or scar tissue, but a soft, feathery, almost lung-like tissue....

Gills!

Joan had metamorphosized[189]. Those webbed appendages of hers had a purpose. She was not a freak. She was just amphibious and never knew it. And now that she had sprouted gills, she could breath underwater.

---

189. *Meaning to change, in fancy science-speak.*

It was a fantastic feeling. As her lungs filled up with water, instead of choking, she felt the water filter through her gills like fresh air. She was going to live.

She took in the water's oxygen and felt her body grow rejuvenated. Energized. Liberated. She felt like she belonged in the water. She never wanted to leave. She kicked off her shoes and socks, and she swam.

The first thing she did was to swim over to Emmett, who thrust Hamlet into her arms. He signaled to her that she should take him to safety.

So, Joan pushed off the sea floor and swam up. Holding Hamlet tightly against her chest, she glided rapidly through the water. Like a tropical fish that had spent its whole life in a tank and was finally set free in the ocean, she rejoiced in movement and swam joyously. She was a creature of the sea and moved gracefully, her webbed appendages giving her tremendous thrust as she glided through the water. She broke through to the surface and deposited Hamlet safely on the edge of the dock, fifty feet away from the trawler.

Nobody had seen her surface. Hamlet would be okay, but what about Emmett?

She had to go back down. She feared it might be too late, that in his selfless act of rescuing Hamlet, he might have killed himself. Yet, she had to at least try to save him.

She dove back into the water and swam. The water flowed soothingly through her gills, and she moved effortlessly through the sea, as though she had spent her whole life underwater. Within a few seconds, she was back on the water's bottom, at Emmett's side. But he was not moving, and he looked dead. She needed to get him out of the water as quickly as possible.

First, she had to free him from the heavy iron chain wrapped around his ankle. But how? How could she save the boy who had saved her just the night before?

Joan tugged on the chain again. Still, it didn't budge. Then, she swam to the anchor. It was heavy, but while underwater, she seemed to have gained a huge amount of strength. She grabbed the anchor and lifted it up easily. Underwater, she was as strong as Marooshka was on land.

Holding the anchor in her arms, she swam around Emmett, kicking her powerful webbed feet as she circled him, literally unwrapping Emmett's foot. It was working. Yes! The chain was loosening. She swam around one last time, and Emmett's ankle slipped free. Emmett was unfettered. She grabbed onto him and pulled him up from the briny depths.

They broke through the water's surface, but instead of hearing the glorious gasp of Emmett's lungs filling with air, she heard nothing. Emmett still did not breathe.

Joan laid him upon the sand at the water's edge. He was blue. Dead. She was too late. Emmett was dead, and it was her fault.

She started to cry. Hamlet rambled over and started howling. Joan had read about CPR in several books and decided to take action. She closed Emmett's nose and opened his mouth. She blew air down into his lungs, while Hamlet banged on Emmett's chest.

Once. Twice.

Three times.

Still nothing. No sign of life. Emmett just lay there, cold and blue and still.

Joan screamed at him, "Emmett! You're the only person I have left in the world! Breath for me! I won't say 'affirmative' ever again if you will just breath! Please, dude!"

Hamlet banged on Emmett's chest again. And then, it happened. A spurt of greenish fluid flew up in the air.

Emmett spit up a combination of baked beans, seaweed and saltwater, all over Joan and Hamlet. But that didn't matter to them; they were so grateful he was alive.

He was breathing again. He was going to live. Emmett was going to be alright. Hamlet hooted with happiness. Joan smiled through happy tears. They all hugged. They were all alive. It was a miracle.

As their group hug slowly dissolved, Joan

looked over at the trawler. It was empty. For the second time in two days, Lazlo must have assumed they were dead and taken off. She looked down the street and saw that, yes, he was already driving the pickup and trailer off into the night. The moonlight bounced off the chrome Airstream as Lazlo and his gang disappeared down the dirt road.

Joan shrugged. She had no desire to follow them. There was really nothing she could do now, but be thankful that she and her two new friends were alive and safe... at least for the time being.

As she watched them go, Joan had a funny feeling this would not be the last time that she, Emmett, and Hamlet would see Lazlo Bleak and his flea circus/side-show gang.

INTO THE GREAT UNKNOWN

Very early the next morning, Joan of Arkansas, Emmett Golem, and Hamlet the Redneck chimp stood above deck on the trawler, leaning against the boat's metal railing.

Dr. Golem was on the dock only a few feet away from them. He had come to pick up the Volvo. He looked up at Joan, Emmett, and Hamlet and said, "Okay, I admit it: I've been too overprotective. So yes, you have my blessing. See the world. I'll take the Volvo home. But before you go... one last thing. Take this, kiddo—" He threw a metal object to Emmett.

Emmett caught it and looked down at it. "What is it?"

"It's a cell phone with a DVD player. I added a fish de-boner, in case you get hungry out there at sea."

Joan smiled and said, "That's very kind of you, sir."

In sign language, Hamlet added, "Fish. Yummy. Tummy."

"Okay, then. You kids be careful and call me every day. Okay? Promise?"

Emmett and Joan both nodded. Dr. Golem smiled, walked off the dock, got into his Volvo, beeped the horn, and waved as he drove off. The three friends smiled and waved back.

This unique threesome was now ready to embark on a voyage into the great unknown. They were a bizarre-looking trio: Hamlet, the

Redneck chimpanzee, the furry, tree-climbing precursor of man; Emmett, the future man, android-humanoid, robotic technological wonder; and Joan, the skinny amphibious girl with webbed appendages and gills, whose big eyes should have been filled with tears and dread, but instead, sparkled with hope.

The three peered out at the fiery sun, glowing hot and reddish-orange on the horizon. The sunlight reflected on the sea, and everything vibrated with life and potential. The saltwater was no longer gray; it had turned sea green, just like Joan's bright eyes.

As Joan turned on the motor and the trawler floated out into the intracoastal waterway, nobody looked back.

They looked forward to the horizon, to the rising sun, and to the great unknown of the rest of their future adventures together.

THE END?

READER, PLEASE BEWARE!

BOOK 2
TALES OF THE TRULY GROTESQUE

HOOK, LION & STINKER

WILL BE COMING SOON...

ANNOTATOR'S NOTE

I, Prof. Odysseus Malodorus, have dedicated my life to trekking the globe in search of the world's most profound grotesqueries[190]. I have amassed hundreds of notebooks and journals filled with sketches and stories documenting the existence of many of the world's most bizarre freaks[191]. For if a human or even non-human monstrosity is rumored to exist, I believe it is my destiny to hunt these creatures down, and, if they are being taunted and/or maltreated, safeguard their existence.

Even though this kind of freak-chasing sounds safer than the cut-throat atmosphere of the academic world that most professors inhabit, it is not. As the world's premiere authori-

---

190. *Mutants, monstrosities and just plain weird looking school-teachers.*
191. *Such as the Minnetonka Milk-Maid, Wanda Schwartz, who had quadruplets and four-matching functional mammary glands.*

The last known photograph of
Prof. Odysseus Malodorus, B.S, M.S., Ph.D.

ty on freaks, I must face death on a daily basis.

Thus, there's a mighty good chance I may be missing, lost or even dead by the time of this book's publication. Yet, please rest assured, no matter what state[192] of jeopardy or decomposition my body may be in, one thing remains certain. All of the events detailed herein are either real occurrences that I have personally witnessed or else, they are true incidents that other legitimate sources have recounted directly to me.

Finally, please note that just because the characters contained herein do horribly grotesque acts, does not mean that you should run out naked in your backyard and try to duplicate these horribly grotesque acts, that is, even if you could. In fact, if any readers of this text even think of attempting to duplicate any of the grotesque oddities contained herein, there will be grave repercussions[193]. Yes, before you can say, Team Malodorus, LLC, its lawyers will hunt you down, sue you for breaking and entering my story, move into your home, and eat all the good cheese in your refrigerator.

---

192. *There is actually a good chance I will be stuck in the state of Arkansas since there is such a high percentage of freaks there.*
193. *It is also rumored that Prof. Malodorus himself or a member of Team Malodorus, LLC, may arrive at your home and give you the longest TIME-OUT in recorded history.*

This book is already written. Your life is still an unfinished text. Make it interesting, fresh and grotesque in your own personal way! Live your life according to what you believe is right and wrong and not according to what some freaking character in a book says or does. Use your imagination to create your own truly grotesque adventures, instead of stealing those featured in Tales of the Truly Grotesque.

-- Stay Malodorus and Truly Grotesque,

Prof. Odysseus Malodorus,
B.S., M.S., Ph.D.

P.S. – I must take a moment to thank Creepy Little Productions for having the vision and the courage to publish this book. **Madame M**, your artistic genius is much appreciated. Without your ability to take my scratchy field sketches and turn them into genuine works of art, this book would not have been possible. Furthermore, this manuscript profited from the keen editorial eye and brilliant mind of the Chairwoman of the Board of Team Malodorus, LLC, **Shana Smith**. Many thanks and many hugs and kisses...

P.P.S. – Even though I am constantly on the move, if you want to try to reach me, your best bet is to go to **www.TrulyGrotesque.com**.

ABOUT THE ILLUSTRATOR

Artist, Madame M has illustrated and written numerous books, including *Creepy Little Bedtime Stories*, *Eerie Little Bedtime Stories*, and *Trauma Queens/Trauma Kings*. She lives in the confines of the barren wastelands in Arizona with her understanding and patient husband, Wolfman Joe and their mischievous offspring, Lili Bird.

Visit us on-line at:

www.trulygrotesque.com

www.creepylittlestories.com

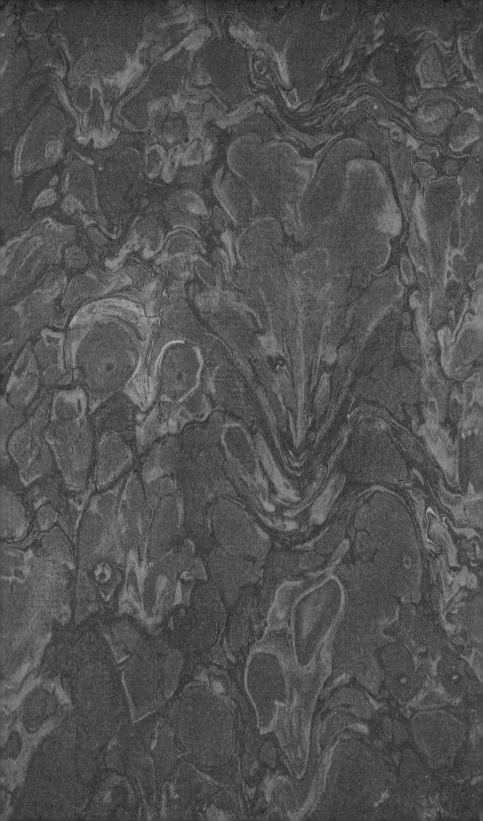